HOW TO GET A
Date

**PAPER
ROAD
PRESS**

Paper Road Press
www.paperroadpress.co.nz

Published by Paper Road Press 2023

Cover art by and © Laya Rose Mutton-Rogers 2023

A catalogue record for this book is available from the National Library of New Zealand Te Puna Mātauranga o Aotearoa.

ebook ISBN 978-1-9911968-8-0 paperback 978-1-9911968-9-7

HOW TO GET A
Date

WITH THE
EVIL QUEEN

MARIE CARDNO

The kiss lasted just long enough for everything to go wrong.

Sian opened her eyes, which was step one in getting things moving from just kissing to any number of next steps. What those might be, with a partner who changed shape with less effort than breathing, she didn't know and was excited to find out.

Somehow, though, with the woman of her dreams right in front of her, it was hard to plan ahead. Hard to think of anything, in fact. Trillin's eyes were a thousand starlit lakes, her skin beneath Sian's questing hands covered with tiny sensory filaments that sought out her touch in return. Feathery cilia merged into scales merged into soft, cool skin the gentle lavender of a sky that hadn't decided yet if it was sunrise or dusk, and all around them—

"Oh *fuck*," Sian gasped, sitting upright.

1

Trillin melted around her and coalesced at her shoulder, her tentacles a defensive wall that circled them both. "Something is wrong? Did the people from your Earth follow us?"

"No." And thank fuck for that, but— "We've got an audience."

They both stared out the tall narrow windows that separated them in this pocket of safety from ... whatever was outside.

There'd been movement. Out the corner of her eye. She was sure of it.

The hairs on the back of Sian's neck prickled. She cleared her throat. "Where are we, exactly? You said a pocket universe, but ... I realise I probably should have asked this before we started making out."

Trillin shot her a mournful look. "Pockets have to exist somewhere. I took us somewhere."

She made a good point. Sian had, in her enthusiasm to be distracted by other things, assumed this particular pocket universe ran on the same rules as the magical university department she'd spent the better part of the last decade studying at. The magical department at Otago existed beneath the mundane campus, a secret cluster of buildings blanketed in a sort of magical fog. The windows of those buildings looked out on misty nothingness. The windows here looked out on misty nothingness. She'd figured it was the same old, and lost herself in the wonder of being able to look at Trillin again without feeling like her brains were about to melt out of her ears.

But what Trillin said made perfect sense. Pockets had to exist somewhere. Their private sanctuary wasn't adrift in some sort of poorly rendered void. They had bumped into some other world and stuck, like a biddy-bid caught on a sock.

Sian gnawed on her lower lip. "Somewhere, huh? Somewhere where?"

"Somewhere no one is trying to exterminate us?" Trillin suggested with more hope than confidence.

They both looked out the windows again. Yep. Definitely movement.

Sian felt the heavy weight of oncoming adventure settle in her stomach.

It would be really great, she thought, if just for *one bloody minute*, the universe would stop throwing new and exciting bullshit at them to deal with.

Which was ironic because up until, oh, forty-eight hours ago or less, she'd been the one throwing herself at the universe. Nothing had thrilled her more than the prospect of more new and exciting bullshit, and if the universe wasn't going to provide, she would be happy to.

Then she'd met Trillin.

Trillin was her – well. She was Trillin. Sweet and curious and sexy in a way that made Sian feel like tweety birds were circling her head. She was a breakaway fragment of the dimension-entity known as the

Endless, who'd done the unthinkable not by breaking away – bits of the Endless were always doing that – but by refusing to return to the whole. She had crafted her own body from lost matter and memories and her own incredible stubbornness.

And if she ever went home, the Endless would annihilate her.

And if they ever went back to Earth, to Sian's home, every other witch in existence would try to annihilate them both. Well. They'd go after Trillin, and Sian planned to stick right next to Trillin, so it was the same thing really.

But they weren't going home. Trillin was alive. She was alive. For one brief, wondrous series of moments, they'd been together in this pocket away from both their worlds. Together and safe.

No grasping tendrils of the Endless or suspicious fellow witch academics squeezing through cracks in the walls. The other fragment of the Endless that had joined them on their adventures, which they'd nicknamed Bunny, had scampered off to nibble on the walls. Sian hadn't really been paying attention. She'd had other things on her mind, and in her arms.

Maybe she should have done a bit more scouting around? Because it was now deathly apparent their sanctuary was more like a pocket inside someone else's universe.

And the *someones else* were enjoying the view.

Pale, murky faces pressed up against windows that had moments-or-more ago looked out on misty nothingness. Whoever they were, they were nothing-ish as well. Colourless eyes and colourless skin. Not human, but not not-human, either. Shrugs given form.

And also kind of like every zombie movie she'd ever seen, when the zombies pressed up against the windows of whatever pub or old warehouse the main characters had got themselves trapped in. "Can they get in here?"

Trillin extended careful feelers. "I do not think so. The spell that formed this room can withstand great force. And they are not ... they are not *trying* to get in."

"So, what are they doing?" Sian muttered.

"Watching us." Trillin manifested a hand and twined gentle fingers around Sian's.

"But *why*?" Sian pushed her free hand through her hair. "I mean, I *know* why. From their perspective we popped up out of nowhere into the middle of their dimension. I'd look at us, too. But—" To her horror, her voice rose into a whine. "Why *now*? When we were in the middle of ... Oh, no. Oh, abso-fucking-lutely not."

The faces at the windows were changing. Colourless skin turned pale purple, or freckle-blotched peach. Eyes like egg whites darkened into shimmering galaxies.

One of them raised a hand and ran familiar-looking blunt fingers through familiar short black hair.

Sian's stomach lurched. "Are we back in the Endless?"

"No." Trillin's voice was strange, and Sian couldn't translate her expression. "This is another world. Not yours, and not the Endless."

"Sure. Right. I was just wondering, because, the … changing shapes to look like us…"

Trillin turned eyes like the hearts of suns on her. "The Endless doesn't *know* our shapes. Not like this."

Fuckity fuck fuck. Had she hurt her by acting weirded out by the locals changing shape, when Trillin was a shape changer herself? But she loved how Trillin changed shape.

Trillin knew that. Didn't she?

"Right! Right." Oh god. Couldn't they get back to kissing? In private. Without the audience. "And there are lots of different dimensions. Obviously." She frowned. "I guess it's one of those things that you know, but don't know a lot about? Everyone knows other universes exist, but it's not like anyone's gone looking. We mostly focus on the Endless at home because of all the uh … invading. I did extra-dimensional studies in undergrad and even that was pretty much all Endless all the time."

All of Trillin's galaxy eyes focused on her. Usually, that was great, but right now it felt like Trillin was more focused on *not* looking at anything else, than specifically looking *at* Sian. She wasn't sure she liked it.

Not that she could blame her for keeping her eyes away from the creatures playing dress-up with their faces outside.

"You learn only about the Endless? That can't be right. Humans have known about many different worlds," Trillin protested in her softly lilting voice. "You travel *everywhere*. I know, because – oh."

Suddenly, Sian had no problem translating her expression.

"I ate them," Trillin whispered. "Maybe that's why you all forgot?"

Sian wanted to claw at her own face. How had they gone from making out to *this*?

And how did they get back?

"The *Endless* ate them," she corrected Trillin gently, hoping her internal chant of AAARGH FUUUCK WHYYYY wasn't visible on her own face.

"I *was* the Endless, when I did it." Trillin's eyes dropped, focusing on what she'd made of herself since then: the tentacles stretching protectively around them both, her hand with all its carefully knuckled fingers holding onto Sian's. Her tendrils tightened and withered away; her fingers retreated. "I don't want to…"

"It's okay," Sian said awkwardly, her words a drop in the ocean of Trillin's obvious misery.

Trillin met her eyes with many of her own. "Is it?"

"If it isn't, I'll *make* it okay." She sounded tough, and certain, and she was almost sure Trillin bought it. She brushed her fingertips along the side of Trillin's face, and frilly tendrils followed her touch.

Out the window, hundreds of fingers brushed along the sides of hundreds of faces. "Speaking of other worlds. Maybe we could visit one? Now? Literally any of them except mine or yours or whatever is out there. This is a bit creepy even for me."

"Yes. We should leave."

Trillin did something. Sian felt the twist of magic, and then the faces vanished. *Everything* vanished, a lurching emptiness that began deep inside her and tunnelled outward, and then everything came back.

The windows of misty nothingness were thankfully empty again now that Trillin had whisked them someplace else. Trillin, *her* Trillin, was staring angrily through them.

"How could they do it so *easily*?" she hissed.

Sian blinked. "Do what?"

"Change. Be *us*." Her tendrils coiled. "It took me so long to make *any* of me, and they just – copied it! Like it was nothing! They didn't even have to—"

She cut herself off so firmly her mouth vanished. A tremor raced along the length of her.

"Pretty bloody rude if you ask me, trying on our shapes without even asking," Sian commented. Ah, fuck. There were emotions here. A whole maze of them. She had to tread carefully. "Want to, uh. Get back to what we were doing before we were interrupted?"

Starlit eyes turned towards her, six at first and then a dozen. "Making love?"

Uh? Uhhhhh? *Be cool.* "If that's what you want to call it. Making – yep. Yes?"

Trillin hesitated, and Sian wasn't in a maze anymore, she was standing on the crumbling edge of a cliff.

You couldn't fire blast emotions. You *really* couldn't. But if you could, Sian would have done it right then, incinerating the sudden precarity of everything inside her.

It had never been like this for her before. Sian had pashed and dashed her way through her teens and twenties with all the sexual subtlety of a sledgehammer. She'd had fun, her partners had fun, and they all went on their way with no one feeling like their heart was about to crack in their chests at any point in the proceedings.

With Trillin – it was different. Wonderfully different. Horribly different. She wanted to discover all the ways their bodies fit together, yes, but – and this was where her roadmap ended – she wanted other things, too. Things so terrifying she wasn't ready to put them into words.

Trillin's eyes did something Sian didn't like at all, sliding off all in different directions, none of them hers.

"I don't want——" she began, and it felt like the end of the world.

"Is it a terminology thing?" Please let it be a terminology thing, she added silently. "*Making love* sounds very – I mean, it means one thing *now*, but maybe if you learnt it a while ago it meant something different?" Not too different, she hoped, but it was already too late.

"It's not *what I want to call it*. It's the only way I know to call it. And I learnt it from eating someone." Trillin's voice was a pale whisper.

9

Every part of her was sliding away now, as though she couldn't bear the force of Sian's anxious attention. "Almost everything I know, I learnt by taking it from someone else. What other worlds there are, or were, and how to reach them. What this body is meant to look like. All the things I want to do with you, and I only know what they are because…"

Her voice failed. Her body was failing, too, falling in on itself, and Sian was paralysed. A frozen statue next to Trillin's anguished dissolution.

She couldn't even see Trillin's mouth anymore, but she must have one, because her voice drifted through the quiet space of their pocket world.

"I don't … I don't want everything I am to be because I killed someone for it."

Is that all? Sian thought, and mentally stared at herself in shock at her own ruthlessness. Murder was bad, obviously, but…

At least she hadn't said it out loud.

Which was probably another bad thing for her to be thinking? Maybe?

Self-examination later. Stopping Trillin from melting into the floor, now. She pushed her self-doubt aside and reached for what had been Trillin's head.

There was little human-looking about Trillin left, but that didn't matter. Sian would have to be even thicker than she liked to pretend she was, not to read the monstrous girl's feelings in this form.

"Trillin?"

A single eye emerged on a thin tendril, and blinked at her.

"You made yourself who you are. And you made yourself who you *aren't*. You chose to leave the Endless. Everything that it was – you remember it. Of course you do. But it wasn't you. It *isn't* you. You're already learning new things that don't have anything to do with sucking the memories out of someone else's brain."

Which – okay, maybe that wasn't the best way to phrase it. Sian winced and tried again.

"Look at where we are now. You created a portal so we could escape Earth without killing anyone to learn how. And you turned the portal into this – this pocket universe. You didn't get that out of anyone's head, did you?"

"Bunny showed me how to do it."

"Sweek!" Perfectly on cue, the other fragment of the Endless poked its head up from a hole in the floor.

"Yeah, and you didn't eat Bunny, did you?"

"I *did*." Trillin's voice was reproachful – but it was more her own voice, as though her vocal cords were returning to the shape she normally made for them. Something inside Sian relaxed. "Then we … un-ate one another."

"And nobody died."

"Nobody?"

Oh. Right. They'd portalled away just as Professor Havers and poor old Jonesy had been doing their best with a destruction spell. "If they blew themselves up, that's their problem."

"And if I was the one who blew them up? If I tore them to pieces as we escaped?"

Trillin was staring at her as though there was a right answer, and Sian had no idea what that answer could be.

"You can't blame yourself for killing someone when they tried to kill you first," she said in the end.

Trillin had a face again, eyes arranged in a fan above that wonderful mouth. But her smile wasn't right. "Can't I?"

Sian opened her mouth to say something that would probably make things worse, when the light changed. The misty nothingness outside brightened, sharpened and revealed—

"Wait." Sian's mouth hung open. "Are we *home*?"

Home. Not the Endless. Which wasn't Trillin's home anymore, anyway. But Sian's hands tightened around her, protective and alert, and she didn't need to take the human's memories to know why. Sian was right: she had begun making her own memories, her own thoughts, woven only from what she had done herself.

And those memories told her very clearly that if this was Earth, then they weren't safe here, either. They only just escaped the last time.

And more than that. Being on Earth, with the way Sian reacted to her when surrounded by the air and magic and history of her own dimension ... it hurt.

Eyes clustered and submerged again on the side of her closest to Sian, sneaking glances at her face. Sian caught her looking and turned her head decisively. Her eyes found all of Trillin's and caught them tight.

"Looks like we're safe in here," she said, more softly than she usually said things. "Even if this is my world again, I can look at you while we're in here, and not scream my head off."

A tiny current of relief washed through Trillin. "Yes."

They would be safe within the confines of this room she'd built from a spell that should have killed them both. It was portal to other worlds and another world both. A miraculous place all of their own.

But it was small. And though she'd reassured Sian that it was sturdy, she did not truly know how much force it could withstand. Would another blast like the one she'd used to create it destroy it, or make it stronger?

How could they be back on Sian's Earth? She hadn't followed any of the worldlines that led there. She had thrown them as far as she could in the other direction. Away from Earth, away from the

Endless, away from *copycats*.

The windows cleared, revealing more of the world outside. It *looked* like Sian's world. Blue skies above and green grass below, with a strip of black concrete in between. Power lines strung between poles like ship's masts. Trees. Flowers.

She tried not to resent the way the words for all these things already existed in her mind.

The grass and the concrete shimmered with the particular shimmer of stillness; countless droplets of water sitting carefully, each in their own place, catching and throwing back the silver-gold light of the sun. A sun like the Earth's sun, which some long-lost and long-recovered part of her had once tried to devour.

Hunger, hot and guilty, coiled within her. *No*, she told it. *That isn't me. Not anymore.*

"Well, it's not like we pitched up right where we came from, at least." A shiver twisted Sian's expression, and she rubbed it away. "I don't think either of us want to see how that ended up. This looks like … I don't know. I mean, one patch of road is pretty much the same as another, right? Look. There's a bee. It's got to be Earth if there are bees, right?"

"But which Earth?"

"Uhh." Sian's expression was wary. Her eyes flicked over all of Trillin's. "Are there … a lot of other Earths?"

The careful way she said it, the fact that she *did* say it, made it easier for Trillin to answer. The Sian who'd entranced her from the moment she had eyes to see her with was straightforward and went for what she wanted. If she started avoiding the truth about what Trillin was now?

She couldn't bear that.

"There were more." *Before me. Us. What I used to be a part of.*

"Still some, though? Looks like it, anyway." Sian peered through the window as though Trillin hadn't just admitted to destroying a thousand versions of her home.

A thousand worlds in which you might have existed, and now never will. Another shiver rippled through her.

Dependable, straightforward Sian was still staring out the window. "How do we tell if this one is mine or another one, then?"

Doesn't it matter to you?

Maybe it didn't. Maybe it couldn't. Trillin knew Sian's world the way a conqueror knew it – but with her new memories, was beginning to understand it, and Sian, in ways she would not have been able to see before. Perhaps there was a reason Sian was such a cheerful blunt instrument.

The Endless had devoured thousands of humans well versed in biting their tongues, and now she managed it herself. She slid to the window next to Sian and extended careful feelers to it.

The transparent material gave at her touch, letting her tendrils peek through to taste the world beyond.

"The air is like your air," she said.

"Great. I'm a big fan of breathing."

"It's ... quiet. Only as alive as your world is."

"Not like the Endless, you mean?"

No, not like the dimension that was one all-consuming, all-consumed entity, hungering and restless. This world felt made of many different pieces, alive and not, in the way that was still so strange to her.

But...

There was something else, at the edge of her senses, but it was too subtle for her to get any sort of grip on it. Something magical? It slipped out of her grasp.

"There's one way to find out whether this is my Earth or not." Sian's voice had a terrible cheerfulness to it. "I'll head outside and see if I lose my mind when I look back at you."

No! Trillin wanted to cry out.

Sian pulled her close for a kiss, and whispered into her skin, "I know. It isn't the funnest way to spend our time. But this pocket universe of ours is a safe zone, right? So, if I start screaming my head off, tangle me up in your tentacles and drag me back inside."

Something in her voice thrummed deep inside Trillin.

"Promise?" Sian prompted her.

"I promise."

If this was Sian's world, then Trillin changing her appearance wouldn't make Sian fear her less, but Trillin still made herself look as human as possible. When she was ready, she nodded to Sian, intimately aware of the interplay of bones and muscles that made the movement possible. As though correct anatomy could save her.

Sian grinned. "First question. How the heck do I get out of here?"

Trillin concentrated. An open arch appeared in the side of the room. The air from outside hit them, cool and fresh and smelling of salt.

"Certainly smells like home," Sian said grimly. She squeezed Trillin's hand, her own flesh so warm and reassuring it was all Trillin could do to keep her fingers from wrapping bonelessly around it and snaring her in place. "All right. Showtime."

Sian stepped outside. Trillin followed her. Staying inside might interfere with the experiment. Sian wasn't afraid of her in there, after all, so they both needed to be outside for the test to be true.

The grass gave beneath her feet, a tiny caress. Her body sang with tension.

Humans had evolved alongside the Endless; their two dimensions had crossed over frequently enough in both their histories that humans had developed an instinctive horror of anything Endless encroaching on their world. Or maybe the horror was what came first, and the Endless took advantage of it. Her memories weren't clear.

Either way, it was a cruel irony: when they were in the Endless, Sian could look at Trillin and her mind remained her own. Like seeing

17

a fragment of the Endless in its usual context made it less terrifying. But the Endless felt her presence, and sought her out to devour her. On Earth, Sian's mind almost broke every time she caught sight of Trillin. And although the world itself didn't want to destroy Trillin, Sian's fellow witches did.

Nowhere was safe. Nowhere except the tiny universe-in-a-room Trillin had created, their bubble between worlds.

Sian's shoulders tensed. "Here goes," she muttered, and turned around.

Their eyes met. Sian's eyes were dark, an intricate web of fluid and flesh. But that was never the most important thing about them. What had drawn Trillin from the start was their energy. The darting, dancing interest and wonder in everything Sian saw. The way her gaze could sharpen or go diffuse, staring somewhere entirely different – and all the ways she could make Trillin feel by turning all those different gazes on her. Precious, and wondrous, a co-conspirator in the infinite strangeness of life.

For so long Trillin had been a part of something all-consuming, never alone because there was nothing of her to *be* alone. Now she was apart. And Sian was who she wanted to be with.

And she wasn't screaming.

"Hey," Sian said, her face breaking into a relieved smile.

"Hello," Trillin replied, awkward with pleasure. Sian's smile turned into a grin. She took Trillin's hands. "I don't think this is my world."

"Because you're not scared of me."

"Because I'm not scared of you." She moved closer, her eyes glittering. "And—"

Whatever she was about to say, Trillin never heard it.

Because a dragon fell out of the sky.

Sian grabbed Trillin and hauled her away. Her mind wasn't twanging with terror. That was a good thing. A massive fucking dragon had just crashed down in front of them. That was a … what the fuck?

A dragon. A *dragon*.

Dragons didn't exist.

Except in this world, they did.

The dragon had fallen heavily. It swung its head back and forth, dazed, and snapped at a picnic table. Sian watched it as though entranced.

It had burnt-red scales and wings that bent like a bat's. The bulk of its body was the size of a bus, but as it hauled itself up on the clawed elbows of its wings, the most relevant part of it swiftly became its mouth full of teeth.

Until very recently, Sian's sister Flora had been the traveller in their family. She'd once sent Sian a photo of herself standing in the jaws of an ancient, giant shark at some museum overseas.

This was like that, only instead of a shark that had died millions of years ago, it was a dragon and it was about to eat her.

And Trillin.

The huge head full of teeth lurched towards them. The great eyes focused in on her with bleeding red intensity.

She called on her magic. A nice, comforting fireball was exactly what the situation called for. And then some running. Straight back into the pocket universe and then immediately elsewhere sounded good.

Her magic sputtered. She stared at her hand as her brain sputtered, as well. No fireball?

"Again?" she cried out, appalled. This had happened in the Endless, too. The world itself had sucked at her magic as she expended it. Here, though...

She tried again, concentrating on the liminal space between *attempt* and *failure* to identify exactly what the fuck had gone wrong.

Her blood chilled.

There *was* no magic.

This really wasn't her world. Back home, witches absorbed magic from their environment and fed it back into the world via fireballs and other, occasionally less flame-based spells. Some places were thick with magic, which posed the usual excitement, or danger, depending on your perspective, and some were in a state of permanent drought, but she'd never experienced anything like this.

It made no sense. This world *had* magic. Evidence: dragon. But it also had a desiccated, swept-clean absence of magic which felt suspiciously like—

"Look out!"

Trillin wrapped herself around her and sprang backwards, gossamer wings billowing out and carrying them away from the dragon's attack. Teeth clashed together with a scream like metal on metal. Sian swore.

Priorities. Number one: don't get so caught up in your thoughts that you get *eaten* by a *dragon*.

She stumbled backwards and found herself on gritty sand. A wall of stinking hot breath washed over her as the dragon drew itself up again. One leg collapsed and it let out a roar that caught Trillin's wings like a sail, pushing them both further back. Away from the road and their portal room. Closer to – the water? Were they on a beach?

Why did this place seem strangely familiar? It was obviously a world like her own – she glimpsed power lines and an asphalt road, with the few neurons not currently focusing on *oh shit dragon* – but from what Trillin said, there were loads of worlds *like* her own. So why did it seem so—

So irrelevant to the question of not being eaten by a fucking dragon? she growled at herself, and planted her feet. "If we can get back inside we can get the hell out of here, yeah?"

"Back inside the room that the dragon is standing beside?"

"Oh…"

Shit.

From the outside, their sanctuary was a ripple in the world. The doorway they'd stepped through into this world almost vanished in the sunlight: a shadow thin as tissue paper.

The dragon's leg slammed down next to it.

Sian made an unheroic gurgling sound. "That's the one. How fast can you get us somewhere else once we're in there?"

Tendrils coiled along Sian's collarbone. "Fast enough," Trillin confirmed, whispering in her ear.

"Any idea where Bunny got to?"

"Still inside."

"One less thing to worry about." The next bit would be tricky. "I'll lure the dragon away. You get inside."

"I'm not leaving you here!"

"No, you're not, because you're going to keep hold of me while you run to where it's safe, and as soon as you're inside you're going to yank me in after you."

"Or I could kill it." Trillin's voice was soft, like something worn so thin it was about to tear.

Sian was in front of her, wrapped in her tendrils. She couldn't gaze into Trillin's eyes, but she could guess what she would find there.

The dragon reared back and roared at something Sian couldn't see. Had something distracted it?

Blood streamed from its flank, a wound she hadn't noticed before.

"You don't want to kill things anymore, remember? Let me help you not kill them." *And if someone has to kill this thing to get us out of here – I'll do it.*

Somehow.

She would do whatever it took to make sure Trillin didn't have to be that part of herself she hated, ever again.

Somewhere behind the swept-clean absence of this world's magic, something turned its attention towards her.

Sian frowned. *What was – oh, shit.*

The dragon lifted its head. It was so unlike anything she'd ever seen before. Such a perfect reflection of everything that a dragon should be – here, in the flesh, in this not-quite-her-Earth. What did that mean? Had the two dimensions split from one another at some point? Had people travelled between the two worlds, bringing stories of giant winged lizards?

She would have loved to stay and find out. Any other time, she would have. How many times had she risked death when it was only her own death she was risking?

But she wouldn't risk Trillin.

She squeezed one of Trillin's arms. "Make yourself as low and small as possible. If the stories that made it to my world are right, it'll be more interested in something human-shaped than something not. Um. Possibly sheep-shaped, too. Don't go all fluffy."

"Sian—"

"Now!"

Sian tore away. The dragon's huge head swung after her. Its nostrils flared.

Fire-breathing, she thought suddenly. *Giant, FIRE-BREATHING winged lizards.*

She might be able to run faster than the dragon could limp-drag itself. Faster than fire, though?

She only needed a scrap of magic. She'd claw it from her own bones if she needed to. Just enough to turn the tide if she needed to, and save them both.

Or only Trillin. Just enough to save her.

Something drew closer, seeking her thoughts like a moth sought fire.

Static buzzed in Sian's ears as she called on magic from her own body, holding it ready for the moment she would need it. The world turned silver-white around her, the morning sun coaxing the damp chill of night into clinging, lung-clogging humidity. Magic came to her sluggishly, as though it didn't want to respond to her call, but it had to be there—

And then it was.

Power clamped down on her like a vice. She had a sudden,

inescapable sensation of being turned this way and that, inspected by a single-minded compulsion searching for ... something.

She blinked. The world spun back into place around her, no longer blinding white but vivid and bright and bruisingly real.

Fire roared towards her.

She flung herself out of the way, hitting the grass and rolling. Heat seared across her back. *Missed me, though.* The air smelled of burning greenery, not flesh.

She leapt to her feet, one arm raised in front of her.

There was a sword in it.

"What the actual fuck?"

The dragon slumped, apparently exhausted by spitting fire at her. Where was Trillin? The shadow-outline of the door into their escape pod was just visible over the dragon's crumpled wing, but Trillin herself was nowhere to be seen.

Sian shouted her name, and a tendril wrapped itself around her free wrist, soft as the dawn. "I'm here."

"You're meant to be over there—"

"No. Something's ... wrong. I don't like it and I don't want to be that far away from you."

"You know, you make it really hard to do the whole heroic sacrifice thing when you hang around trying to save me back," Sian grumbled through gritted teeth. She hefted the sword. It glinted in the sun. "Do you know where this came from?"

"That's what's wrong," Trillin said quietly. "And him."

"Who?" Her ears were ringing. The sword was *heavy.* She tried to drop it, but her fingers were locked in place.

"Foul beast! Your reign of terror ends here!" A male voice rose above the buzzing in Sian's ears. "No longer will you – will you—"

Sian stared. The man was in his late twenties or early thirties, she guessed, with brown skin and the rumpled, slightly mad eyes she knew well from late nights at the library. But that wasn't the thing that really drew her attention.

Another sword? He was wielding it like he actually knew how to use it. A real sword. Long and shiny and pointy.

He pointed it at her, and his voice shook. "You."

"Seriously? Point that thing at the dragon!"

He came towards her, sword still unhelpfully aimed at her heart. "Another prince. Finally. You can—" He winced and clutched at his forehead, dark curls falling over his hand. When he looked up again, his expression was stricken. "No. This doesn't change anything, does it? Shit. It doesn't…"

"Look, mate, I'm not here to get in your way." She waved her own sword in what she hoped was a conciliatory manner.

He straightened as though jerked up by invisible marionette strings. "Take heart! Together, we will vanquish this creature!"

"What?"

Trillin's voice trembled. "Sian, we should leave. *Now.*"

There was a tremendous groan. Huge wings battered the lawn. Shit on a stick, the dragon was still alive.

Sian leapt back, putting herself between Trillin and the dragon.

Its eyes cracked open. Blood-red irises filmed with torn sclera stared unseeing for a moment, then focused on the sword-wielding maniac.

Smoke poured from between teeth the size of fenceposts, and then the man lunged forward. Silver carved an arc through the air. Blood spattered, smoking where it sprayed across the ground.

Sian's heart thudded in her ears.

No more dragon.

No more sword, either. The weight in her hand vanished the moment the life left the dragon's eyes. Whatever that meant, it had to be bad, especially since the fucker who'd killed it still had *his* sword.

Sian backed away, drawing Trillin with her. Whatever was going on here, she would prefer to figure it out from the safe distance of way the fuck somewhere else.

But the man had other ideas. He turned to them, his sword bright and bloody. "You!" he called imperiously. "Who are you? Do you come to aid my fight, or to challenge me?"

"Sian—" Trillin whispered urgently from behind her.

Yeah, she got it. They were in trouble.

The man strode closer, his eyes narrowing. "Who's that hiding behind you?"

Trillin shrank back. Sian didn't blame her. Anger pulsed through her.

"Who's asking?" she shot back.

He drew himself up. The sun shone through his hair in a way that Sian was pretty sure the sun didn't usually do, making his dark curls appear dipped in gold.

So *that* was where this world's magic was.

No wonder the world felt so scraped-clean. Magic clung to the man in front of her like it did to the natural environment in her own world. But—

Trillin was right. Something was wrong. He wasn't using magic.

It was using him.

Her eyes narrowed. "Get back inside, Trillin."

"I can't. It's gone."

"What?"

"The dragon landed on it."

Fucking fuck. "Can you make another one?" The madman with a sword was still stalking towards them. Sian backed away, keeping herself between Trillin and the stranger.

"It took so much energy, the first time. All the power from the annihilation spell."

And this world didn't have enough juice. Or if it did, it was tied up in whatever the hell was happening to Mr Golden Highlights over there.

"Long have I quested in search of the monster who kept my love from me. Now the beast is slain, and I..." His voice wavered. Something like terror flickered in his eyes and for a moment, the golden light that surrounded him faded. "My princess – she is – *shit*, she's not here, is she? When did I – when did that thing—"

"You killed this dragon for some princess? What does that make you, Prince Charming?" He looked the part. Shiny hair. Shiny sword. The flickering terror didn't quite fit, though.

"The dragon's dead. I should be..." His eyes hardened and he raised his sword, pointing it over her shoulder. "I see now. That – *creature* behind you..."

"Sian!" Trillin's voice was even more urgent. Her tendrils split and lengthened, wrapping desperately around her wrist. Shit. If this asshole killed a dragon, what would he think of Trillin?

"She's *my* princess," Sian growled. The words sounded right. They *felt* right.

Her hand curled around something that wasn't there; an invisible weight, waiting for her to pick it up again. Not the magic she was familiar with, but... "Back off."

"Princess? She looks more like—"

"Watch yourself," Sian growled. Anger ratcheted in her chest. It had to be anger, because what was the alternative?

Bunny had been in the portal room. And now Bunny was gone. Their way out of this world was gone. She'd dragged Trillin out of the

29

Endless into a series of worlds that wanted to kill her, and for what? So she could keep making things worse for them both?

There has to be a way out of this. The guy had a sword. Was that how it worked in this world? Goodbye fireballs, hello pointy slab of metal?

If only she could do something. Save Trillin, the way Trillin kept saving her, over and over, instead of being so goddamned useless.

Be better.

Be the hero.

It wasn't a spell. It wasn't even a wish.

But the magic heard her.

Trillin recognised the hatred in the man's eyes. The Endless had loved this moment, in as much as any of the variations of *hunger* that passed for its emotions felt like love.

He hated her, and soon that hatred would be hers.

No. That wasn't her. Not anymore. Sian's colleagues – they'd hated her, too, with the seething brightness of fear, and she hadn't devoured them.

She might have killed them, though. Was it any better, killing someone and not eating them?

And she might have to kill this man. Here, in this world that rang with the absence of magic, a lack that scraped across her edges.

Something is wrong.

Which was a dangerous thing to know, almost as dangerous as knowing it and wanting to know *what* was wrong, because the best way she learnt things was by pulling them apart and making them part of herself. The few things she'd learnt by experience alone paled in comparison to the weight of what the Endless had learnt through invasion.

In front of her, Sian squared her shoulders, bone and muscle and sinew moving in perfect partnership. Trillin kept telling herself she didn't know how that worked, but the truth was she didn't *let* herself know. The knowledge was there, inside her. Waiting for her to pick it apart the way the Endless had picked apart the bodies the knowledge had come from.

Maybe if she took apart the man with the sword, she would understand this world better. Find out where it was hiding the power she needed to create another portal-sanctuary and escape.

Something brushed the edges that separated her from the world around her, so soft that at first she didn't notice.

That would work, wouldn't it?

Though – why had she thought this world didn't have magic? There was magic all around her. And Sian. And the man with the sword. It roiled through his veins, burning and freezing. If she could tear it out, it might be enough that she could make a portal so they could leave—

Leave?

Magic, faint as dust motes in a sunbeam, drifted into her body, into the glowing core of her mind. Something that wasn't a person, was barely more than a bundle of intentions, wound itself around and inside her.

No. She couldn't be allowed to leave.

"Don't worry about who's behind me. She's shy. Who the fuck raised you, that you're saying shit like that about people you just met?" Sian squared up, making herself as big as she could between the man and Trillin. Trillin would get the idea, right? Stay hidden behind her until she could … something.

If the next step of this plan could make itself known, that would be really good about now.

"I…" The man blinked. His shoulders dropped, and then the sword did, which was the best thing Sian had seen all day. "It's dead. Isn't it?"

Sian glanced over his shoulder at the extremely deceased dragon. "Yep."

"Is it—" He swallowed, paling. "Still a dragon?"

"What else would it be?"

"That's what I'm worried about." He gave a thin smile. "Still a dragon. That means it can't be – god." The sword fell from his fingers and disappeared before it hit the ground. He put both hands over his face.

Whatever is going on here, this place is fucked up. "Right," she said out loud. "Well, I'll leave you to clean up. We were just passing through, so—"

"Wait." His head jerked up. "You saw all this."

"Uh … yeah."

"But you're not—" His eyes narrowed. "Are you?"

"Not what?"

"I'm not trying to cart you away over my shoulder, so you can't be a Princess," he said dryly. "I'm not trying to kill you, so you're not one of *them*. But you weren't any help slaying the dragon, either."

She rubbed her fingers over the strange, empty weight in her hand. "Was I meant to be?"

"How do you do it? You can see magic, but you're not affected by it. Tell me how." He came towards her, desperation twisting his face. "You have to tell me. If there's a way out of this that isn't *that*, I need to know. I can't keep doing this—"

"What, killing dragons?"

"Killing *any of them*. Dragons. Monsters. It never ends, and the only way to *make* it end is—"

He stopped. His eyes shot past her to where Trillin was hiding – *please let her still be hiding* – and something in him hardened and relaxed at the same time.

"Oh," he said dully. "It is another monster, after all."

"Wow. You just don't fucking stop, do you? Trillin isn't a monster, she's—"

Sian turned and her voice faded away.

The Trillin she knew was a miracle of undulating forms. Even at her most human-looking she sprouted odd fronds and tendrils or too many eyes. When Sian breathed, her lungs expanded, her chest rose and fell. When Trillin remembered to breathe, scales rippled across her skin, unfurling into wings that tasted the air.

This wasn't her.

It looked like her. But it wasn't.

For a moment, she was back on her own Earth, staring into the face of the woman she lov—*liked*, let's not get ahead of ourselves here when this shit was scary enough already, thank you. But she had stood in front of Trillin, and everything she'd *liked* about her flipped a switch in her brain and turned into a terror that tore her mind apart from the inside.

But this wasn't like that, either. This wasn't mind-destroying terror. It was a far deeper fear, the same one she'd read described in old records of Endless incursions. The sudden certainty that the person you knew was gone, and something else had taken root behind their eyes.

Something was wearing Trillin like a suit.

"Trill—"

Black tendrils shot out and wrapped around her neck. Sian choked and stumbled back. Beside her, the prince struggled as tendrils throttled him, pushing him to his knees.

Sian tore away. The thing that wasn't Trillin released her, and the smile that stretched across Trillin's face wasn't hers.

"Trillin? What's wrong?" She had to believe she could still hear her. "Did the Endless follow us here?"

"Nothing's wrong." Trillin's voice was full of shadows. "The magic here is … different. That's all. But I think I can use it. I—"

She shuddered and broke off. Her shape changed. She became taller, her edges more defined, her angles sharper. A crown of dark shards appeared on her head.

Her eyes flicked dismissively over the man, who was still on his knees, lips parted as he clawed the tendrils from around his neck.

Then she looked at Sian.

The voice wasn't Trillin's. This thing wore her body, her ability to change her form, but it wasn't *her*.

But the eyes were. Brilliant and lustrous and shimmering with the same fear that had flickered from the prince's as he slew the dragon.

Help me, her eyes pleaded, or maybe, *Run!* The tug on Sian's heart came again, harder this time.

This wasn't her friend. Her would-be date, or fling, or any number of more terrifying things. This was a creature that spoke to something inside her that cracked open like a shining rock, and spoke in return.

It was a queen. A monster, like the dragon whose rampage the other Prince had quelled, but more powerful.

I have to destroy it, Sian thought, her lungs clenching with sudden desperation. She stepped forward, hand wrapped around the hilt of something that hadn't been there a breath ago—

And then darkness rushed up around them all.

When it faded, Trillin was gone.

The thing inside Trillin felt like her own thoughts. When she tried to talk to it, it repeated her words back to her in the same voice she used to speak to herself in her own head, but it … wasn't her.

Wasn't her?

But…

She wriggled, trying to make herself comfortable within her own body. The body she had made for herself. It felt different. It felt like she'd never had a body before.

…She hadn't thought that. That wasn't her thought. Except…

This body is … new. A new beginning.

36

Yes. A beginning. That was what this reminded her of. Wonderfully and horribly familiar, like those first moments after she fragmented from the Endless and discovered what she could do, be, as her own person—

Curiosity blossomed inside her, listening with wordless, polite hunger.

Not her. Someone else, becoming.

You didn't need a body to be afraid. Trillin hadn't realised that, until now. The same way she hadn't realised until this very moment she no longer had a body. The magic that had poured into her as easily as she changed shape filled her right to the edges. She could no longer feel where her form ended and the world began. She could barely feel where her mind stopped and the other entity's—

Quicker than thought, she raised walls between herself and the intruder. She'd almost been too late. Its curiosity clung to her mind, strange echoes of her own thoughts and ... something else. Something new, and becoming, but old, too. Something that was running from a tide of dread so great it had seen no way out until it had found her, but it hadn't known it was running, hadn't known it was afraid, until it crept beneath her skin.

Who are you? Trillin thought at the being in her head.

It did not respond, but it tried, the same way it had almost succeeded at when it first entered her, to tell Trillin that it was a part of her and not a stranger.

That it would all be okay, now. Everything would work out.

I do not think so. I have been many things. I would know if I had ever been you.

And none of the things she had been had ever wanted to rid themselves of what they absorbed, until her. The Endless, the many previous fragments who had freed themselves and been taken back into that ravenous whole – they had all wanted to become more. Never less.

She wanted to be herself and even more than that, she wanted *not* to be whatever this was.

Her instinct was to pull it to pieces. No. Not *her* instinct. The instinct of what she had once been. Her own becoming had been such a slow, experimental process, ravelled up by the knowledge that if the Endless noticed what she was doing, it would take her apart.

She could take this wisp of magic apart. See what it was made of. But once she did, it wouldn't be itself anymore. It would be part of her.

Forever.

She couldn't risk it. It was already too close to being every part of her.

She knew how to kill things. To take them apart, piece by piece. Become them. Have them become her.

And she knew something else, now. Knew it by the complicated admixture of the memories of everything she had once been, and her new ability to see and learn about the world, and what she'd gleaned from the intruder before she peeled herself away from it.

The scraped-clean emptiness of this world. The way magic clung to Sian and the dragon and the man with the sword. Whatever was inside her needed them.

Something was wrong here. This world's magic was twisted and hungry. Not the way the Endless was hungry, but it wanted something from the humans that lived here. It had made its world a wasteland in pursuit of it.

And she wasn't the only one it had in its claws.

"Where did she go?"

"Your friend? Oh, shit. Your friend. She…" The man looked like he'd stepped in something nasty. He lifted one hand – the one without a sword in it – and for one awkward moment, seemed like he was about to pat her shoulder.

She snarled at him, and he dropped it.

"*Where did she go?*"

"That's a more complicated question than—"

Useless. Something from this world had taken Trillin. She had to get her back. She had to save her—

—save her—

The same way Trillin had saved her, over and over, since Sian dragged her away from her life.

A very small voice inside her reminded her that by the time she turned up, Trillin was already separating from the Endless and therefore elbowing her way into plenty of danger already. She ignored it.

Whatever had Trillin, it had teleported away. Teleportation left tiny tears in the fabric of reality. She could use that. A tracking spell—

The world spun around her. When it stopped, she was on hands and knees, the taste of copper in her mouth.

Right. Shit. No environmental magic. But she couldn't be running that low on magic, could she? She must have some left in reserve.

"What did you just do?" The maniac with the sword again. He came towards her, eyes wide. "How did you do that?"

"Fall on my arse? Gravity." She pushed herself to her feet. "Back off, sword guy."

He stared at the sword as though he'd forgotten about it, then held it down and away, his mouth twisting. "My name's Victor—"

"And you kill dragons. Got it."

He went green. "That's not exactly…"

"I don't care about exactly. I care about where my – where Trillin went. So if you can't tell me—"

"I can't."

"—stop wasting my time. I have to find her—"

40

"And what? Stab her through the heart?"

She felt it. The sword's point halting as it met bone. The strength she put behind the blow to make it a final one, an *end*, and the way that force echoed back up her arm and into her own chest.

She stumbled back. "What the hell was that?"

Victor sighed. A line of gold glimmered around his forehead, and he cast a sour look over his shoulder at the dead dragon. "Magic. Look. I'm sorry about your friend. But this has never happened before. I need to talk to – oh. Great. Here she is."

He couldn't have sounded less enthusiastic if he tried.

"Victor!" a woman growled from behind Sian. "What the hell do you call this?"

He winced and swore under his breath. "Hello, Rosamund."

"All over the city? You killed it out here, you couldn't have started the fight somewhere out of the way, too?"

"For the – if I could have spent my entire day so far doing anything *but* taxiing around after a bloody dragon, I would have."

The woman continued as though he hadn't spoken. "On a *Monday?* Half my tenants had to call in sick to work!"

"You let them out of the tower to work?" Victor muttered, backing away.

"Excuse me? You know I can hear you when you do that, don't you?" The woman – Rosamund? – stalked past Sian, casting a quick glare her way as though she hadn't given her permission to exist yet.

41

The sunlight glinted off her sleek silvery blonde hair and, weirdly, off something tucked into the thin line of her mouth.

Rosamund turned her sneer back on Victor. "You – *ugh*." She paused to spit something into the travel cup she held in one glossy manicured hand, and what clinked into the mug didn't look or sound like phlegm. It *sparkled*.

Sian stepped forward. "Hey," she said. "What're you—"

She didn't manage to say anything else. Rosamund half-turned towards her, reaching a hand palm-out only a few inches from her face to ward her off. Victor shouted a warning.

Everything went … soft. And shimmery.

Motes of golden light danced around the princess's head. How had she not noticed the glimmer of gold on her forehead before – the faintest hint of a tiara, gleaming with precious gems? Emeralds and sapphires and cloudy diamonds echoing the same shades in her eyes, which were no longer glaring dismissively, but – how could she have thought this vision would glare at anyone? Her face was made for joy.

An ache filled Sian's heart, sweet and wistful. "My lady," Sian breathed, too reverent to speak her name aloud. "You—"

"My prince." Rosamund's voice was soft, which was so much the opposite of everything she had seen of her that – what was she thinking? It was completely right. Of course she was soft, and sweet, and all things lovely.

Rosamund's hand turned, as soft as the rest of her, palm-up, waiting for her to clasp it.

Eternity trembled in Sian's heart.

She raised her own hand – callused, work-roughened. Everything her princess's was not. But there would be no more hardship, after this. No more striving. No more lonely desperation.

Their fingertips brushed.

And pain lashed her eyes. She stumbled back, clawing at her face. Someone had thrown gravel at her?

"What the fuck?" She blinked, stared out uselessly through stinging waterlogged eyes, wiped her face again, swore again. Victor had another handful of stones ready. She threw her hands up at him. "What the *fuck*?"

"You're welcome." He dropped the gravel, his shoulders loosening.

"Why did you—" She broke off as she caught sight of Rosamund.

The other woman was a metre or so away, staring at her still-outstretched hand like it had rotted to ash in front of her. Her sleek hairdo was all scuffed up; her sneer faltered.

"Oh god," she muttered, and didn't even try to hide the gemstones that fell from her lips. "That was too close."

"Try not shoving your hand in people's faces, then," Victor suggested.

Rosamund sniffed, regaining some of her former sneering self-confidence. "How was I to know she was a prince?"

"By looking at her for more than half a second?"

"Wait," Sian said, with the sensation that she needed to barge into the conversation now before it ran away without her. "I'm not a prince."

They both stared at her. Victor groaned and rubbed his forehead. Rosamund smiled the smile of someone who would spend the rest of the day filling up on wine and telling herself it was self-care. It was nothing like the gentle joy that had lifted the corners of her lips when—

"What was that?" Sian burst out. "You were – we almost touched, and then – what the hell was it?"

Rosamund's smile thinned. "True love."

"Like fuck it was!"

"Yes, well, in this case, I think we can both agree on that." Rosamund spat a mouthful of gemstones discreetly into her travel mug, and Sian pointed at it, making a noise that even to her was incoherent. "Oh, good god," Ros continued. "You have no idea, do you?"

"No! That's why I'm asking. Because—" Sian broke off. "It wasn't real. Whatever spell you just cast on me to make me feel like that wasn't real. That means that what I felt when I looked at Trillin—"

She turned around, searching with the aimlessness of panic, but there was no sign of Trillin or the strange shadows that had taken her away.

"It wasn't real," she repeated to herself. Maybe if she said it enough

44

times, the sick feeling in her stomach would go away.

She'd looked at Trillin and hated her. Feared her. Not like she'd feared her when she looked at her back home on her own version of Earth, like she was a creature of vast and terrifying power and Sian was a mere ant in front of her. Which, fair, Trillin *was* a creature of vast and terrifying power. It was one of the things she liked about her, when she wasn't trying to peel the skin off her own face about it.

This had been different. For one horrifying moment that hadn't been horrifying until it was over, Sian had looked at Trillin and thought *she* was a bug that needed to be squashed. That if only she were gone, the world would be a better place.

"It felt so real," she whispered.

"It always does." Rosamund had regained her sheen. She cast Sian a look that was almost friendly in its condescension, and sighed. "First time?"

Sian's head hurt. "First time what?"

"First time finding yourself a princess."

Behind her, the corpse of the dragon stared blankly at the sky.

Something inside Sian snapped. "I've been in this world less than ten minutes and so far I've been attacked by a dragon, had a *sword* appear in my hand out of nowhere, and had a fucking love spell cast on me? What is wrong with this place? Where did Trillin go? Why won't you explain what's going on?"

Rosamund's perfectly sculpted eyebrows came together. "Oh,

come on. Even if this is your first time, it must make some sense to you. The feeling that it's all falling into place?"

"What sense? What are you talking about?"

"*Is this the end I've been waiting for? My happily ever after?*"

Her voice was flat, but something in Sian soared in response. As though the words had been waiting inside her all along. She swallowed.

"Welcome to the club. Victor can fill you in on the details. I think I'll keep my distance, all things considered." Her eyes skated up and down Sian, obviously unimpressed. "I'm sure you have hidden depths. *Very* well hidden. Good luck finding a princess better suited to – whatever it is you're bringing to the table."

Sian didn't have time to decode the first bit of that. "I'm not looking for a princess. I already have someone. I'm looking for *her*."

"Oh, well, even better. Lucky you, knowing her even before the—"

"It's not another princess." Victor had been so silent, Sian almost forgot he was there. She wished he'd stayed that way. He sounded too grim for whatever he had to say to be good news.

Rosamund's eyes daggered to him. "What do you mean?"

"There's something new. It appeared as soon as I killed the dragon."

Sian got the feeling Rosamund would have rolled her eyes, except that it was beneath her. "If you're not going to get the girl, then you have to keep slaying the monster. You of all people should know that."

Victor was not above rolling his eyes. "Oh, thank you for saving me from a fate worse than death, Victor. Now hurry up and shackle yourself to your own unhappily ever after." His voice sobered. "This one didn't appear out of nowhere. It took over a person. Like us."

Rosamund's lips had been pursed over a fresh mouthful of sparkles. At Victor's words, her whole face slackened in shock. A faceted sapphire hung wetly in one corner of her mouth. "Not a person. That doesn't—" She grimaced and spat into her cup again. "That doesn't happen. The monsters are meant to make sure we stay on our given path. They're – temporary. Why would the magic do that to a person?"

"Why does it do this to any of us? And it doesn't matter that it's never happened before. It's happened now. And the next time the magic wants to pair two of us off—" Victor thrust his hands deep into his pockets. He looked sick. "A *person*, Ros. Not a – a thing. I don't know if I can…"

"Well, you don't need me to tell you what your other option is. Maybe this is what you need to stop shilly-shallying around. Or … maybe it's not your problem at all." Rosamund stared Sian down with her jewel-sharp eyes. Sian tried her best to meet her glare for glare, but it was like the ground beneath her feet was crumbling. "You saw your friend change. The magic has you, too."

"Uh – yeah? I saw what happened. It's not like she turned invisible. But what do you mean, the magic *has* me? I have *magic*. I'm a witch."

Rosamund scoffed. "You're not a witch. You might look like something the cat dragged in, but you're not *that* pathetic." Sian must have looked even more confused, because she sighed and added, "It's tried to make human-shaped monsters before. Witches. Old women waiting at wells, that sort of thing. It could never get them quite right. They've always been … strangely disturbing."

"More disturbing than everything else about this place?" Sian burst out.

"Mmm." Rosamund inspected her carefully. "But – you're sure?"

"Sure of what? My magic? I—"

"Sure you wanted to kill her. Your friend."

"No. No, I—"

"She definitely did?" Rosamund was talking to Victor, now, as though questioning Sian had been a formality. Less than a formality. Sian wanted to storm over to her, wanted to do anything, but if she moved she might fall and never stop. "This might not be all bad," Rosamund went on, talking to Victor in an undertone. "There hasn't been more than one monster at a time for years. And this one seems to have chosen her as its enemy Prince. If it stays alive, maybe the rest of us can have a – a respite." For a moment, something weary and hopeful flickered in her eyes, then her nostrils flared and it was gone. "She obviously won't want to kill her friend. If we help her, keep them apart—"

Sian tried to shout to get their attention, but the humming in her ears was suddenly so loud she couldn't hear anything over it and the sound of her own breathing.

It couldn't end like this.

It had barely *begun*. Sian would never call herself sentimental – no witch worth their salt would, given the attrition rate – but the idea of losing Trillin scraped a raw wound open within her.

If she thought about it too hard she might realise the wound was so raw because it had been scraped open so many times, but she wasn't going to think about it that hard. Or at all. Witches were famed for picking holes in the universe, but some doors were best nailed shut.

Anyway, she was going to save Trillin. No door-opening required.

Everyone kept talking about happy-ever-afters? Princes and princesses and monsters? They had it wrong, calling Sian a prince. But if anyone was her princess, it was Trillin. She just had to find her.

My happily ever after, Sian thought, and the words made something twist bright and horrible and wonderful inside her.

Somewhere close by, Rosamund scoffed. "Don't worry. I've no intentions of snaring you away from your beloved."

"You're not the one I'm worried about!"

They were sniping at each other like they were up in each other's faces, bristling for a fight. But as sarcastically heated as their argument got, they were careful to keep a few metres apart.

The love spell had hit her when she got too close to Rosamund.

If the same thing would happen with Victor? No wonder they were keeping their distance.

She closed her eyes, pushing Victor and Rosamund's voices out of her mind. She'd hoped one of them might tell her what the hell was going on here, but – no. She didn't have to rely on them. She *couldn't* rely on them. Wasn't that what her life had taught her? If you waited around for other people to help you, you'd be waiting forever.

If you want something, for the love of god, grab hold of it before the universe took it away for good.

A tracking spell. That was what she needed. Something niggled at the back of her mind – she was running out of magic, yes, she *knew* that, but she could manage this, couldn't she? It couldn't have been that long since she recharged. Or even if it had, she must have something left in the tank or she wouldn't have got up again after that last attempt at casting.

Anyway.

Eyes shut. Shape the spell.

The magical emptiness of this world scraped against the inside of her skin. But it wasn't all empty, was it? The emptiness was what was left behind by the entity that had taken Trillin, and taken all the magic of this world as well. A bottom trawler eating up everything in its path.

Stillness was not one of Sian's top attributes. But she let her consciousness spread out, wifty-wafty like before she figured out how to roll herself in magic and turn it into a stick to poke things with, and it turned out the world here wasn't completely scraped clean. The trawler had left scars in its wake.

And—

Suddenly, she knew where to go.

Ha ha, she thought, grimly. *Found you.*

But … something was wrong. She shook her head. She'd barely drawn on her magic at all. This felt like something else, pulling her towards it.

And do I trust this sudden and convenient knowledge? she asked herself, already knowing the answer.

She opened her eyes. Victor and Rosamund's argument seemed to be winding down. Maybe now was a good time to try and find out more about what the fuck this world's deal was, but—

I have to save her.

The words tolled inside her, echoing in the hollow of her chest.

Time to go.

No fanfare. She just turned and went. Along the road that wound strange and familiar between the hills and the water. Towards a turn she knew was ahead – up the hill, through the trees. To … She had it, almost, but it escaped her.

It didn't matter. She had to go there. To save … to save…

She clenched her fists, and didn't notice the pressure of a ghostly hilt against her palm.

Everything was dark. Not the darkness that was the absence of light; the darkness that was something stealing her sight away from her. Trillin twitched extra eyes into existence.

They didn't appear.

Nothing did.

And still the magic boiled through her, formless but – no. Not formless at all. There was a shape there, overlaid upon itself so many times she couldn't count it, self-replicating and slippery. She hunted it through herself and every time she thought she had it in her reach, it was no longer there and was everywhere around her.

What are you? she asked. Something just beginning. What had it been? What would it be, now?

There was no reply.

Shit started to get weird around the first bend in the road. Not that it wasn't weird already.

Weird in the immediate why-are-the-houses-turning-into-trees sense, though, not the what-is-wrong-with-this-entire-world sense.

The houses were turning into trees.

It started at the corners of her eyes. Wood cladding crumpling into bark. Children's bikes and abandoned gumboots shivering into shrubbery, chimneys stretching branches like skeletal fingers towards the sky. Doors becoming gaps between towering trunks. If she looked straight at them, they turned back into houses and fences, empty car ports gaping wide – *Where is everyone?* – but the moment she looked away, the forest returned.

And then it switched. She couldn't tell whether it happened suddenly, or so slowly she hadn't when it changed and she began walking through trees, with the houses ghosts at the edges of her vision and the road only a memory beneath her feet.

"Okay," Sian huffed. "That's fine. It's—"

She blew out another breath and it came out in a plume of fog.

"…It was not this cold a moment ago, right?" Sure, she was shivering, but she'd kind of put that down to her batteries being so flat she could barely see straight.

No one replied. There was nobody around to reply.

People must live here. Right? In the houses. There had been a café or shop or something by the beach, too. How did that work, if the houses were trees now and people were still living in them?

Or not.

And that wasn't the only thing. None of it was the only thing. There were so many things. And underneath and on top of it all the strange familiarity of the place kept itching at her, as though she *should* recognise where she was, and if only she took a moment to stop and get her bearings—

No.

She couldn't stop. Not until she'd done what she needed to do.

Sian narrowed her eyes, and—

Did *not* poke magic at her surroundings to figure out if this was a pocket universe like the one she and Trillin had escaped Earth in, or a sensory spell overlaying the physical world, or a brain worm making her think she was walking through a winter wonderland while her body was lying comatose in the gutter.

Because whatever fucked-up enchantment had mind-whammied her the first time, it had struck right after she tried using magic. And now it was leaving her alone. She wanted to keep it that way as long as possible.

Also, she kept edging away from thinking about just how much magic she had left inside her, which, along with how much she hated acknowledging that was what she was doing, was a good indicator that she was in some fucking trouble. Expending any power at all, especially if it was power she *did not have*, was a recipe for lying comatose in the gutter all under her own steam, no nefarious enchantments needed.

If enchantments even worked like that here. If it was an enchantment that had affected her, and not…

She glared suspiciously at her hand. It was still empty. But the memory of the sword in it was heavier than a memory should be.

"I shook it off," she muttered to herself. "It hooked into me when I tried to use magic. If I don't use magic, it doesn't have anything to hold onto."

That weird shit with Rosamund had faded when she got far enough away from her. The same with the … feeling she didn't want to think about. When she'd looked at Trillin.

Get too close, use too much magic, and the happy-ever-after thing would take hold again. Stay an arm's length apart, don't go trying to throw fireballs, and everything would be fine. The spell had probably worn off Trillin by now, too, so all they had to do was find each other again and come up with a way to scrape enough power out of this dried-out husk of a world to go home again. Or anywhere but home. Anywhere but here or either of their homes, and they would be fine.

…Probably.

She shook her head. There would be time for poking holes in this world's weird magic shit later. Or, even better, no time at all, ever, because she and Trillin were far, far away, enjoying a sunset or beach or star-watching or some other romantic shit.

"I have to believe that," she murmured to herself.

"Believe?"

All the chill in the air got together and grabbed the back of Sian's neck. She spun around.

Behind her was the queen.

A storybook queen. An evil one. A day ago, Sian couldn't have said what an evil queen looked like, but now she knew as strongly as if it were written on her bones. They looked like this. Tall and regal and the only living thing in the world, magic coiling in towards her like water down a plughole.

She would have known Trillin anywhere. But this wasn't Trillin. Not anymore.

The queen had skin the colour of human skin, wrapped over a human frame. Sian's heart sank. Even the coronet of black shards that ringed the queen's head like a halo of night looked like something that had been built, not grown.

The figure tipped its head to one side. It smiled. The movement of its neck was perfect; its smile was perfect.

It was all wrong.

"You're not Trillin." It barely even looked like her. Somehow that made it worse. It had taken her body and made it over like a thrifted dress. "Who are you?"

Her fingers twitched. *No fireballs*, she had to remind herself. *Trillin is in there. Somewhere. And if you zap her body, we'll have to go back to the Endless to get some more for her, and nobody wants that.*

"Trillin?" the figure said. "Trill-in…"

Sian's jaw twitched. "You're in her body, using her magic, and you don't even know her name?"

The queen's eyebrows rose. Her lips curved red and dark around the words as she repeated, "Be-lieve. Trillin."

Sian stopped.

The queen formed words again, silently this time until half a word came out on a slow breath "—lin." Her eyebrows jumped again.

"...Are you even listening to me?" Sian crept forwards. "Hey!"

The queen stared at her. Her eyes were perfect, human eyes. There was no trace of the gentle shapeshifter in them. There was no trace of *anything* in them. Nothing alien and nothing human.

Nothing alive.

Sian's heart kicked.

"Trillin, are you in there? Can you hear me?" She had to believe that she could hear her. So long as Trillin was still alive, she could save her.

Save her. Her own unvoiced thought seemed to echo through the winter all around.

The queen's eyes were still staring blankly into her own. "There is nothing for you here," she intoned, her voice like snow falling.

"You think I'm going to believe that?"

"You are so alone." The queen's eyes sharpened, as though she were peeling away Sian's thoughts, layer by layer. Something tugged at her heart. "It does not have to be this way."

"I wasn't alone before you kidnapped my girlfriend, you—" Sian took an unheeding step forward, peering more closely at the queen. "Parasite. That's what you are, isn't it? And that's what *this* is." She spread her hands, listening to the strange tug inside her. Not her heart. Her *magic*. This was where all the magic in this world had gone, sucked up by a parasite. She wasn't sure where the swords came in, or why Rosamund spat sparkly stones, but she could figure that out later.

Because right now, the parasite was feeding on Trillin.

"Your princess is not here, Prince."

"I'm not a prince," she muttered. "Or a hero of any sort. Really. You've got that bit wrong."

Sian sketched out the spell she needed in her mind, hunting around inside herself for the power she needed to fuel it. Oh. This was bad. Being low on magic was one thing, but now she was forcing herself to actually look, there was so little she had to do the mental equivalent of licking her pinky finger and squishing it into the corner of a cake tin to pick up the last crumbs.

It would be enough. It had to be. Grind it down, smear it around the structure of the spell.

This so-called queen was a magical parasite. It would take more than one witch to exterminate it, but if she could detach it from Trillin…

The spell was ready. She steadied herself, hand outstretched to cast, but her mind was already zigzagging off. Once Trillin was free there was still the issue of not having enough magic to create a portal, what with all this world's magic being tied up in the parasite and its various … hosts? Symbionts?

The parasite had scraped the world clean. They would need to scrape it back. Steal or harvest it from poor bastards like Victor and Ros, or that dead dragon down by the water, or—

Kill the Queen.

Magic surged. She charged forward, her sword hand swinging around in anticipation of the weight that settled in it. Metal flashed in a silver arc. The queen stepped sideways, but she was ready for that. Desperation tore at her heart. The world was broken, the sky ablaze, but here was an enemy that could be defeated. A way to find her happy ending.

The spell to detach a magical parasite from its host was a simple one. It didn't need much juice, just enough to lure it away with promises of more tasty magic elsewhere. Then you grabbed the victim and ran.

She pivoted, planted her feet, thrust—

Ran where? a voice inside her head asked, and Sian smashed into the fact that her plan wasn't, actually, at the same moment she realised she wasn't casting a spell.

She was thrusting her sword through the Evil Queen's chest.

Trillin's chest.

Their eyes met. The perfect blankness of the Queen's gaze shimmered. Sian waited for there to be some sign of Trillin in them, waited unbreathing in the stillness of terror, waited for a glimpse of burning galaxies and ancient stars; a sword couldn't kill Trillin, Trillin didn't bleed red blood, this couldn't be happening—

The Queen's eyes froze over, black like they'd been colored in with permanent marker, and then shadows drew in around the perfect human shape of her body and she was gone.

Sian stumbled.

Her sword was red.

"No!" she screamed, and everything went black.

Trillin stilled. *What was that?*

Something had happened. But she was so far inside what had once been her own body that she didn't know what. Her eyes, her ears, all the sensory equipment she had created to interact with the world were no longer under her control, and the being that had taken up residence in them wasn't letting anything through. As though her body was a blanket around her mind, hiding the world from her.

The being didn't answer.

What happened? she asked again.

"What … happened?"

The voice rattled at the edges. But it was a *voice.* Not an impression, but words, thrumming through skull and jawbone to the secret place where Trillin was hiding.

And the presence felt different, too. The thoughts pressing up against the barrier she'd formed between it and her held a different shape.

She uncurled her own thoughts a little, concentrating. *Something happened. What did you do?*

It had teleported her body away from Sian. That was the last thing she remembered. The last time she'd been able to reach her body's senses and see or hear the outside world.

But there was more to existence than the world that existed outside. The body that had so recently been hers was shivering. Something that wasn't quite a memory hovered at the edge of all the being's thoughts; the cold, the dark, the damp, the suddenness of red flesh and white bone where a breath ago had been life.

Trillin had seen terror a thousand times. Had, very recently, known it herself.

Was trying not to feel it now.

What's wrong? she asked it. *Why are you doing this? What do you want?*

Want? It did not want anything. It strove to fulfil its purpose. And now, with this body, it would be able to do so. Before now – before it found this body—

And suddenly it was talking out loud again, with her mouth. "Before, I always made a monster for true love to defeat. Now I have a body! I don't have to send the monster off and hope. Your body will make sure it works properly. *Every* time."

When did you become an 'I'? thought Trillin, and didn't say anything. Nor did she say anything as the being kept talking with the body that had been hers, its stilted voice smoothing out, becoming breathy with excitement.

"You are the last piece I need. A monster that can restore itself, and try again, and again. A monster who has *thoughts*, and not just—" The words broke off, replaced by a complicated impression of pouring magic into solid form, over and over, until there was no longer enough magic to pour, and it had to scrape magic thin over the bones of old enchantments. "I made them easy to defeat. An evil that could be destroyed so it would never destroy them. So they could be happy. Not like…"

Confusion buffeted against Trillin's defences. More emotions it didn't know what to do with. Didn't know how to stop the body it had stolen from letting them blaze higher and higher. She almost felt sorry for it.

"But it didn't work. They defeated my monsters, and still stayed apart. Lonely. Here. *Everywhere.* Everywhere, when they were left with nothing, they could have had everything – This way will work better. They cannot just kill *you* and escape. You can stop them!" The voice sounded exultant, now. "Make sure they keep true to their love! Let them find a better ending, the ending they have been waiting for!

Let this not be the way it ends, ever again!"

This what? Trillin wondered. Beneath the creature's words was a river of something like terror, dark and deep.

"Stop them running away. Stop it from taking so *long*. Show them that they need – that they must – that they should *want*—"

Dread and longing made it breathless. Trillin saw and felt a hand outstretched – knew, somehow, that the hand had never found what it reached for, but saw overlaid all in gold a picture of the hand grasping another, of lips meeting. Of a moment that lasted forever, joyous and bright.

So that's what you want. Trillin let her thoughts drift out soft and diffuse into the part of her mind the being had stolen into. *You want the people here to find their happy-ever-afters. You want them to destroy a monster, and fall in love because of it. You want them to destroy ME, over and over, as a mark of their love.*

"That isn't *want*. And I – *I'm* not an … I. I'm not…"

You may not have been, before, Trillin told it gently. *But you have a body now. These things happen, with bodies. They exist, and they change the way you exist, too.*

She reached out, her presence as soft and diffuse as her voice had been, a breath of mist within the pulsing warmth of her flesh, and made one tiny change to the body the invader had sunk into, not knowing the risks of corporeality.

I'm not going to do any of those things you want, she told it, her voice disguising what she was doing. *Because this isn't my body, anymore. You've taken it over. It's yours. YOU will be killed, over and over, until whatever purpose it is you long for is fulfilled.*

"I am not—" the being protested, but it was too late. The body it had worn like a cloak closed around it.

Explosive sensation. A kaleidoscope of sights and sounds and tastes and touch overwhelming from the outside and a dam bursting within.

"I don't want anything," the being protested, tasting the salt air on its lips, tasting the meat of its own tongue in its mouth. "No – what is—"

Unless you leave now, Trillin told it, softly, softly, letting the parasite's own fear at all the new sensations drive it to where the air kissed her skin.

"It hurts," the parasite said, its mind trying to flinch from the body it had stolen but trapped by the same edges Trillin had drawn around herself as she made her own shape for the first time. "It hurts! Make it stop!"

Then leave, Trillin told it. *Go back to what you were before.*

Almost – almost – there. Muscle by muscle, blood and fat and epidermis, she coaxed her body back under her own control. The parasite was still there, twitching like a fragment newly split from the Endless. She just had to find a way to flick it off. Perhaps she could frighten it into a far corner of herself; it was already pulling

64

away from as much of her as it could, from the pain – yes, there was pain, but right now it was useful pain. She might have to sacrifice the piece of herself it was lodged in to really be rid of it, but that would be worth it.

If she couldn't make it take itself away. Peel out of her flesh as easily as it had sunk in.

Go now, she repeated. *I won't be your monster. And this way you don't need to be, either.*

"I can't!"

You don't want to be the monster, dying over and over. Believe me. Trillin hardened her voice. Her body was almost entirely hers again, now, as she filled the space the parasite left behind as it cringed away from the pain. There was … a lot of pain, actually.

Which was new for this body, but not new for her.

I remember so many deaths. Nothing is worth that. Go back to what you were and fulfil your purpose another way.

Do it, she pleaded silently, because otherwise I will have to kill you to get you out of me and that isn't how me killing things works. If I kill you, you'll be a part of me forever.

The parasite's thoughts were crumbling as its body sang its existence: pain and pleasure and strangeness. Trillin had had so much time to become used to the sensation of being in the body she'd made for herself, and had the memories of other bodies to prepare herself and compare it with. But this creature was new to fleshy existence.

What had the entity been, before it stole its way into her body? There had been a moment before it struck – a breath, or a closeness, of something formless and yet shaped with intent.

There were pieces of Trillin that had been pieced together from scholars who might have known about such things. But—

I want Sian, she thought, misery sending shoots through what was left of her. She wanted the light in Sian's eyes, the enthusiasm with which she launched herself at questions, so that it was not her alone here, trapped in her own hard-won body, finding a way to kill this person who had only just begun to be.

"There is no other way! The magic is almost gone. When it runs out—"

Trillin didn't hear what would happen when the magic ran out, because that was when she regained enough control of her body to notice the hole in her chest.

She stared at it, wanting to make more eyes to stare at it, as though that would help, as though that would make there be something other than blood, blood she was sure she hadn't made so red. Or so much of.

What??

"See?" Her lips moved, but it wasn't her voice that came out. "There is no leaving. No going back. We are already a monster."

How did this happen? She reached for the wound, spun the spilling blood into shining threads and wound them back into herself, knitted flesh and skin over the hole until she was whole again.

"A Prince. You see? There is no going back."

A Prince? What do you mean?

It meant Sian. She had some control of her body back now, her defences against the intruder pulled like a too-thin blanket around the trembling core of her remaining self. Her body remembered the sword. Her eyes remembered the hatred in Sian's gaze as she swung the sword.

"Yes," said the parasite, exultant. "That prince. The one who will kill us. Over and over, until she finds her true love."

Black softened into shadows, into the red glow of light behind closed eyelids, and juddered sickeningly into the haphazard blur of reality. She was a lump of pain with a central nervous system that had gone into catastrophic meltdown. She was … *ouch.*

Nearby, a man was talking, his voice low and hurting.

"Don't joke. You joked about dragons last time, and guess what showed up here?" He paused, and Sian just made out the tinny shape of words on the other end of a phone line. Whoever he was talking to exclaimed in shock, or outrage – she wasn't sure which. "It's like it's listening to us. Not a natural phenomenon like we thought. It's – it's paying attention. Changing."

Another pause, and he added: "It's a person now. No. Don't – it hasn't latched on to me. Don't come. Christ. The magic hasn't given up on our happy-ever-after yet, but it hasn't come to *that*." Another listening pause. "There's a woman here who's friends with the woman who got … transformed. She's a prince."

Whoever he was talking to swore like someone Sian wanted to be friends with.

"I know. Ros had some ideas, but…" He sighed. "Just when you think things couldn't be worse, right?"

This was getting awkward. Sian flung out one hand. It hit something that thudded to the ground, and in the time it took her to convince her eyes to open, he was in front of her.

The guy from the beach. The dragon-slayer.

She nodded to him. "Hey."

"You're up? She's up," he told the phone. Sian stared at the coiled wire connecting it to the machine on the wall. What decade was this world in? "I'd better go. Don't worry. I'll leave the saving the world to her. I'm just here to sulk and look pretty, remember?"

The other person said something that sounded like, "And don't you forget it."

Victor smiled. "Miss you," he said, so quietly Sian almost missed it. A pause while the other person replied, then, "You too."

Sian tried to speak. Cleared her throat. Tried again. "Where am I?"

Victor stared at the silent receiver for a moment, then sighed and hung it back on the hook. "Don't worry. I brought you back to my flat."

Why? she wondered, on top of everything else she was wondering. "Who was that?"

"Someone I care about." He hesitated, sighed, and added, "Tash. She's my princess."

"Oh. Congrats?"

"Not really."

His words didn't make sense, but not much did, so. Everything was all … woozy. The sort of woozy that was the equivalent of someone saying, Oh no, don't look over there, everything's fine but don't look, except the *over there* they were trying to keep her attention away from was everything from her neck down. She didn't need to look. She could already feel it, and it felt like someone was taking a cheese grater to her bones.

She tried another question. "Back to your flat?"

"You're welcome. And – I'm sorry. About what happened down the bay." His face twisted. "You needed our help and I ignored you. Not exactly princely behaviour."

She snorted and shook her head. Mistake. For a few nauseating seconds, the world slammed against her senses. When it settled, she took in more details. Late afternoon light slanting through a window. Shelves of books, some actual pieces of furniture, some planks stacked on old bricks. The smell of old takeaways.

And her, presumably. Here, also. Bodily, though still in that woozy way that was bad news. She looked down.

She was all there. So far as she could tell. Lying on a sunken sofa upholstered in faded orange corduroy, and some idiot had put a granny square rug over her knees. She surreptitiously kicked it off as she sat up. "Forget it. What, uh. What happened after that? How did I get here?"

Victor was hovering over her, arms folded tightly over his chest. So … this was his place? His granny square blanket?

She really didn't want to know that he was the sort of guy some-one had made a blanket for. Or the sort of guy nobody had made a blanket for and he'd had to buy it, sad and alone, at an op shop. Or that he'd crocheted his own. She didn't want to know anything about him or his fucked-up world; she just wanted to find Trillin and leave.

Hadn't she … been doing that? She'd had – not a plan, exactly, but…

"How much do you remember?" he asked.

Great. The sort of answer that made you feel *really* reassured. "I remember—"

She'd been mostly sitting up but also mostly slumped against the sofa's deflated cushions, but now she bolted upright. Panic wrapped iron wires around her heart. Trillin. Oh, god, Trillin.

"I killed her."

"You definitely didn't kill her." Something in his voice made her search his face. He looked away, his head turtling into his shoulders. "Trust me. I've seen those things – sorry, not things – I've seen them die before. You didn't kill her."

"You followed me? You and your fucking magic sword? You could have hurt her!"

"No chance of that." Victor shuddered. "The dragon was bad enough. One bout of heroics per day is my limit. And even if I had got close enough to do anything, it wouldn't have made a difference."

"What's that supposed to mean? She's not – she can't be—"

She didn't want to remember, but the memories surged forward, slow and thick. How her plan to cast the parasite removal spell had left her head so quickly it was like it had never been there in the first place. How picking up the sword hadn't even required thought. Only action.

She'd always had a stubborn pride in her ability to do things without letting thoughts get in the way.

And she hadn't thought a single thing as she stabbed the queen through the heart.

Trillin. She'd stabbed *Trillin.*

Her mind jerked between half-formed thoughts until it spider-webbed something that was almost a complete thought.

She had been wrong. This world's strange enchantment hadn't left her. She wasn't immune, looking in on this world's magic from the outside. Whatever made people here act out some sort of fucked-up fairy tale play was a parasite, and it had infected her the same way it did everyone else.

"I thought I could save her," she whispered. "I didn't – I can't have—"

"She's not dead," he repeated, louder this time. "She – you'd better see for yourself."

Sian was already mid-lurch. He caught her, his shoulder unsettlingly bony beneath her arm, and helped her stumble to the bay window at the end of the room.

The world outside was wrong, and so familiar Sian's skin crawled. "Wait," she said, not so much to Victor as to the universe, begging it to slow down. "We're in Dunedin?"

He shot her an odd glance. "Where did you think we were?"

"I don't know, mate, I just fell out of the sky." She stared out the window again, willing the view in front of her to change. "I figured travelling between dimensions meant you ended up somewhere different, not – another version of where you already were."

That was definitely Otago Harbour. From the other direction from where she normally saw it, but still. "We're on the peninsula? Which means that's—"

Home.

This world's version of it, anyway. The hills low and slumbering above the shining water. How similar was this world to her own? Somewhere over there might be the house she'd grown up in. The house she'd shared with her parents, while they were still alive, and then her sister and aunt.

The university. Hell. What did her department look like, in a world where magic turned people into fairy tale puppets?

Except it wasn't the department she was wondering about. Was it? In a world so similar to her own, but where the magic was different – where a parasite had changed how things worked…

She swallowed. "What is it I'm looking at that's meant to prove Trillin's alive, here?"

"Other direction."

Sian turned her head. "Oh."

This way, the window looked out over a few spindly fruit trees, a half-hearted garden, and beyond, a hill that stretched up into tall trees and creeping mist.

Piercing the mist was a castle that looked like the glass-shard coronet worn by the creature who had stolen Trillin.

"The fuck?" Sian asked, for lack of anything else to say.

"You didn't kill her." It was good news, but Victor said it like a death sentence. "She disappeared and, a day later, that appeared." He paused. "It's over Larnach Castle."

"That's not Larnach Castle. I'd remember the spikes."

Victor made a frustrated sound. "It's the magic doing it. I've never seen anything like it before. Sometimes princesses have powers that affect their surroundings – you'll see some of it in Ros's tower – but nothing of this scale."

In Sian's world, Larnach Castle was nothing of the sort. It was a nineteenth-century construction complete with crenellations, turret and ghost, and the only invaders it ever saw off were those who wouldn't stump up the entrance fee. She confirmed with Victor that it was the same in this world.

And Trillin was there. Or the queen was, and she had to believe that was the same thing, the same way she had to believe her sudden need to storm outside and rush towards the mist-clad castle was something she could fight.

Her fingers tightened on the windowsill.

Victor took in her gritted jaw and white knuckles. "You wouldn't be fighting off that sudden desire to head over there swinging your sword if she was dead."

"Good. Great. Thanks. I'm so glad to know that."

"It gets harder the longer you keep it up. That's how the dragon got me, yesterday. I barely woke up before I was scooped up for an adventure."

Go there. Defeat the evil.

With effort, she turned to face him. "What the fuck is going on?" she asked. "The basics. Please. Explain like I have two brain cells and they're both hungover."

And she would listen, the way she should have waited and listened the day before instead of letting this world's magic and her own terror

74

take her to confront the queen without knowing all the facts.

He sighed. "Magic is real," he said, with the gloomy intonation most people saved for telling children that mum and dad weren't going to live together anymore. "You're living in a fairy tale, now. You're a prince; whenever you meet a princess, you'll fall head over heels in love with her. If you can get away in time, it won't stick. If you can't—" He shrugged eloquently. "Congratulations. You're going to live happily ever after."

"Like what happened yesterday. With what's-her-name."

"Ros?" He nodded, and paused, like he was waiting for her to catch up.

"But that's not all, is it?"

His jaw worked. "You're not surprised to hear that magic exists."

"No. We have magic where I come from, too. It just works differently there."

"Where you come from?"

"Another dimension. A world like this, but different. It's not important."

"It's *not* important? Fine. Well, however, magic works where you come from—" *The loony bin*, his expression said. "Here, it's all happy-ever-after."

"No offense, but … does 'happy' mean something different here? Because when you said that, it was like you were describing someone dying."

One corner of his mouth pinched in tight. More of a grimace than a smile. "Hah. No. Do you have fairy tales in your world?"

"Uh, yeah."

"Think of it like that. In a fairy tale, you have a handsome prince—" He gestured ironically at them both. "—and a beautiful princess. They lock eyes across a crowded ballroom or lost shoe or whatever and get their happy-ever-after. But a prince needs something to do before he can win his princess's heart, and that's how you get—"

"Monsters." Sian's voice didn't sound like her own.

He nodded.

"And what do monsters do?"

"Fuck knows. You'd think they would lay waste to the countryside, or something, but not that I've seen. It's like they don't exist until you look at them. And when you do – when *we* do…" He raised a hand, fingers curled around the hilt of an invisible sword, and let it drop. "You saw the dragon."

"I saw you kill it."

His mouth twisted. "I never thought I'd be grateful I only had to kill dragons."

"What do you mean?"

"Monsters are just that. Monsters. Beasts. You get too close to a princess and next thing you know, some creature with too many teeth turns up, and you hack at it with a sword until it's dead. Or sometimes they skip the you-see-a-princess step altogether and just try to lure you closer to one. The dragon was trying to gnaw its way into Ros's tower to get one of her tenants when I arrived and I make a point of staying the hell away from that place." He hesitated. "Do you understand? The story works in threes," he said slowly. "One prince. One princess. And one monster. You slay the monster, you get the girl."

"What if my monster is the girl?"

"Oh, well, you're fucked, I guess. Just in a new and interesting way."

"Wait." Her brain was clutching at straws, now, and this was the one it came up with: "You said the person you were talking to on the phone right now – she's your princess? You *have* a princess? Your happily-ever-after person?"

She remembered the grief that had cracked his face when he woke up from the princely enchantment that had made him kill the dragon, and wondered what could be worth putting yourself through that, time and time again. "Why isn't she here?"

"Because we actually like each other." He stared at her like she was three steps behind, which, to be fair, three was probably underestimating it. "You've experienced the other way around. The magic telling you to hate someone you love. Now imagine actually – actually liking someone, but every time you get within two metres of them, you both turn into someone else. Like characters in a play. And there's nothing you can do to stop it, and you're still in there, behind your own eyes, and *she's* still there behind hers, and if you don't get away from her you'll spend the rest of your life with someone who isn't – isn't her. And isn't you."

He turned away. "You must be hungry. I'll get you something to eat and we can go see Ros."

She was starving, but a sort of starving that didn't stop at her stomach. Even her bones felt parched. Scraped as dry and raw as the magic-empty landscape outside, as though her body needed something more than food.

Victor disappeared into the next room. Sian stood at the window, trying not to think about what he'd said in a way that didn't hurt too much, and trying not to think about why her bones felt like they were about to disintegrate, when something he'd said bubbled up in her mind.

"What do you mean, that castle appeared a day later? A day later than what?"

He leant back around the kitchen door. "A day after you went to find her. You've been asleep for almost three days."

Soon, the creature said, with an anticipation that set Trillin's entire being on edge.

78

They drove past the dragon on the way to meet Ros. Sian stared at it longer than she wanted to. "Is it ... dissolving?"

"They always disappear after you kill them. Eventually." Victor approached driving with the same grim pessimism he approached everything else.

"And you just leave it there? No one minds?"

"No one else can see it. Only us. The same way no one else notices if you start swinging a sword around. Or *that*." He jerked his head in the direction of the mist-wreathed castle and Sian resisted the urge to dive out the door and charge up the hill towards it.

She gritted her teeth. "Where are we going?"

"The meat market," Victor said.

"The what?"

He sighed. "Ros's place."

It made sense, Sian thought a few minutes later, staring up at the building Victor had parked outside. At least, it made sense if you assumed anything in this world made sense.

The evil queen lived in a castle. And Ros's princesses lived in a tower.

The closest thing you got to a tower in this city, anyway. The train station, a colonnaded gingerbread palace complete with bell tower.

"People live in there? What, everyone gave up on trains in this dimension, too?"

"It was converted to apartments a few years ago. Ros bought the building after the refit."

"And uses it to house princesses." She glanced sidelong at him. "You have to tell me if I'm going off track, here, because it all sounds equally fucking weird to me. I can't tell if I'm talking shit or not."

He ignored her. "Ros knows we're coming."

"You'd know. Didn't you call her?" He had called her, right? Because from everything she'd learnt about this world so far, turning up unexpected in a building full of the type of people who made your brain go cuckoo seemed like not the greatest idea.

Victor's jaw was tense. He muttered, "Everyone else will be upstairs."

Ohh. Right. He wasn't talking to her. This was a personal pep talk.

"You all right there?" she asked, eyeing him.

He nodded shortly. "I won't lie to you. Being here isn't my favourite thing." He looked up at the building, its frontage of limestone and black basalt. Sian felt a strange dizziness. It looked too close to the station in her own world, the local rock too similar to stones that made up the university buildings around her own campus. And if the buildings were the same they must have been designed by people who were the same in this world as they were in hers, built by the same people, lived in by—

Nobody lives in the railway station at home. Not even trains, most of the time, she told herself, stamping down on further thoughts before they could root themselves in her mind. Even if their worlds had been similar at one point in the last few hundred years – or less, maybe, when was the railway station built? *Stop thinking about it.*

There was no reason for them to have stayed that way. Not with the magic here being the way it was, and the magic in her world being the way *it* was. Doing the things it did.

There was no reason to think there was anyone here she would know. Not even people who, in her world, were dead, but maybe in this world—

She swore under her breath. *Stop thinking about it.* Since when did she have trouble with thinking too much? It had to be this world getting to her. Or the strange, hollow itchiness under her skin where her magic should have been.

The almost-there weight in her hand, where the sword wanted to be.

She swallowed and jerked her head towards the station. Fuck's sake, even the flower gardens out front were the same as in her world.

"This is a good idea, right? Being here? There isn't – I don't know. Something else we should try first?"

"What do you feel like trying?"

Finally. Something she didn't need to think about. She didn't need to see it to know where it was. Beyond the roads and buildings, past the water, the—

She growled in mixed frustration and anguish as she realised what she was staring towards.

"Yeah. Sorry. It's like that." A muscle in his jaw twitched. "I know it's like throwing yourself into the lion's den. But nothing like this has ever happened before. A person being the monster … Ros and I agreed it's best we do something before anything worse happens."

"Like me stabbing her through the heart?"

"Like that."

Victor gave her a tight grimace that was so far from a smile she wanted to wince. "When we go inside, remember that Ros had to get in arm's reach of you for the magic to take hold. Keep that far away from her and anyone else you see, and you'll be fine."

"What about you?"

"The radius gets wider the longer you put it off. Just don't be surprised if I spend this meeting scuttling around the far walls." He set his shoulders. "Okay. I can do this. Let's go in."

He marched from the garden path to the colonnaded entranceway and pushed the doors open, head hunched between his shoulders like a turtle. Sian followed, her neck aching in sympathy.

Thank fuck she'd never spent much time here. Outside, yes, at the weekly farmer's market, and her aunt had brought her and Flora here once for an art exhibition in one of the halls upstairs, but the station's interior wasn't familiar enough to keep her insides lurching.

Everything inside was limestone and tiles; functional on the walls, intricate mosaics on the floor. She could imagine the letters to the editor, expressing prissy relief at the developer not destroying this piece of local history. Whatever else Ros was, she hadn't stooped to sledgehammering the mosaic steam-engine in the middle of the floor.

A stairway led up to the mezzanine floor and, she supposed, whatever rooms had been converted into living spaces. She had a sudden image of the same hall that had hosted the art exhibition, refitted for exhibiting princesses instead, and felt slightly nauseous.

It was as bad for them as it was for her, right? Being at the mercy of this magical parasite. What was the point of it? What did it get out of doing this to people?

"There you are."

Ros stalked out of nowhere, apparently, clad in a silvery two-piece suit that made her look more like the offspring of a dragon and a knight than a princess. "You're awake? Good. Victor explained how this is going to work?"

Sian folded her arms, her defences rising as fast as her hackles. "He explained how the birds and the bees function in your fucked-up world, sure."

"Let's get started then. I surveyed the girls. A few of them are more desperate than I'd thought, even considering you might be telling the truth about being from a different world. There's a shortlist on the—"

"Wait. You surveyed them? For what?"

Ros blinked slowly at her, like a cat changing its assessment from *potential threat* to *big idiot friend.* Or just *big idiot,* frankly. "For your princess," she said slowly. Something sharper than the stones falling from her mouth glittered in her eyes. "You didn't think I would just let you at them, did you?"

"Let me at them?"

"Climbing the battlements. Storming the castle – no, that's what we're trying to prevent, isn't it? Hacking your way through the hedges." She wasn't bothering to hide her gemstones anymore; they clinked to the floor with every word.

"What hedges?" Sian clung to the desperate hope that she didn't know what Ros was talking about. She'd come here because Victor said they could help, damn it, not— "What the hell are you on about?"

"Vines, hedges – I'm not the scientist in the family." Ros's nostrils flared as she inhaled. Sian's head was spinning. She breathed in, unconsciously echoing the other woman's inhale – oh, god, that had better not be another fucking prince thing, was it? – and was about to say something dumb and rude when the scent hit her like a truck.

Green. Like someone had boiled up the scent of growing, creeping things until it was so concentrated she could taste it on the edges of her tongue, underlaid with a sweetness that hurt.

She blinked, and in the split second between the shadow of her eyelids and her eyes opening again, the ticket hall was full of rose vines.

Her skin went cold. From everything she'd seen of this world, there shouldn't be magic here, but...

It had to be another princess. Ros had her sparkly stones. She was pretty sure there was a fairy tale about a girl who spat jewels when she spoke in her world, too. And one who spat frogs and creepy crawlies. Roses. That was...

"Sleeping Beauty?" she burst out.

Ros's perfect eyebrows shot up. "Aurelia. *That's* an idea."

"You're shitting me." Sian's voice came out a combination of flat and strangled. "There's actually someone in here who's cursed to be asleep until – until what? Some twit with a sword stumbles over her? And you want *me* to be the twit?"

"You—"

"That is *fucked up.*" Sian ran her fingers through her hair. "So – what? She just wakes up and I'm the first thing she sees? She falls in love with me, or the prince version of me, and loses everything about herself? I'm asking this theoretically. There is no way in hell this is going to happen."

Ros made a frustrated *tsk* noise. Something clinked behind her teeth. While she was busy fishing it out, Victor cleared his throat.

Great! Someone else for her to yell at.

"This was your plan to help me? Pair me off with someone in a *coma?*"

"Sometimes happily ever after is the lesser of two evils."

At least he sounded like he resented the words coming out of his mouth.

Sian headed for the door. "I'm sorry if your friends are desperate to leave the single life. Or the sleep-your-life-away life. But my priority is getting Trillin away from here."

"How?"

"I'll figure that out when I need to."

"By killing her again?"

Ice washed through Sian's veins. "It didn't kill her. Remember?"

"And how many times do you think you'll be able to do it before you wish you were killing yourself, instead?" Victor demanded. His shoulders were still hunched, but when she stared back at him, he was glaring at her with anguished determination. "I told you outside. This has never happened before. It's never been a person, let alone someone any of us know."

"So we're an 'us' now?"

"You'd rather be on your own?"

I'd rather have Trillin back! she wanted to scream at him. Her fists clenched, empty and useless.

"Neither of you seem keen on your own happily ever afters. How can you stand there and tell me to let some magical parasite lobotomise me?"

Ros frowned. "Parasite?"

Victor got in before Sian could explain. "Neither of us is facing the same risk you are. I can stay away from my princess and we'll both be safe. Ros can reject everyone she sees on principle the moment she sees them, so long as she keeps her distance. But you're connected to your monster. So long as you're both alive, she'll be a problem you need to solve. And princes only know one way to solve problems."

Sian licked dry lips. "What if I could go back to my own world?"

"Right. Your own world." He ran one weary hand down his face. "If you can leave, what's to stop you coming back? It's only delaying the inevitable."

Unless I can get rid of whatever the parasite infected me with while I'm home, Sian thought. But that didn't actually solve the problem, did it?

Victor was right. The problem wasn't her. The problem was Trillin. And she couldn't be solved with a sword.

Nausea twisted at her gut. She let her mouth talk while her possibilities danced in her head. A slow, grim dance. "I don't think I could leave, anyway. Coming here took a lot of magic. Magic your world *doesn't have*, unless I'm going to do some sorcery of the sort even my world frowns upon and boil up your bones to leach it out."

Victor went slightly pale. "Good thing that wasn't an option to start with."

"Your other option isn't much better. How is me shacking up with some poor coma patient meant to get Trillin out of here?"

Ros's eyebrows pulled together. "I understand you feel guilty for the part you're unwittingly playing in her fate, but—"

"But what?"

"You can't do anything about it. None of us can." Victor's tone was leaden.

"So I'm meant to just give up?"

"It's better than destroying yourself!"

Sian blinked, taken aback by the snarl in his voice. She stared at him for a moment, longer, then Ros. Then both of them.

Realisation struck, hideous and clear. "This isn't about her, is it? You're worried about me. You're concerned for how this is going to end up for *me*."

"I know you're worried about your friend." Holy shit. Ros's voice was actually *gentle.*

"You want to save her. We've all been there."

"But what's happened to her has never happened to anyone before. We don't know if there's anything left of her to save. But *you* are still here."

"Still salvageable," Sian said weakly. Like a wrecked boat that just needed a lick of paint and off it could go, ferrying a parade of princesses. "You don't get it. This isn't about me. I don't want a princess, I want—"

So many things she was only just finding names for, too late.

She groaned. "I can't leave her here and go home, and I can't nope out and go off into the sunset with someone else. I have to save Trillin."

"That's the prince talking." Victor's tone was low and bitter.

"No, it's me, the stupid fuck whose fault it is she's here in the first place!" she growled. "This isn't about getting a happily ever after. It isn't about any sort of *ending*."

A shiver went through the other two, and she felt it tugging at her own skin. The magic the parasite had planted in them, responding to that word again. Why?

She didn't have time for that. None of them did.

"I don't want to save Trillin because of how I feel about her. I do, but that isn't the biggest problem. I need to save her because I'm the reason she's here and if I can't save her, she'll save herself." She stared at their uncomprehending faces. "Trillin isn't some helpless maiden. She's a sexy baby nuke. I have to save her because the alternative is her freeing herself, and if she does that you're all fucked."

There was a long pause. Victor's brow furrowed. "What's a nuke?"

"What's a – *aaargh*." Sian tore at her hair, eyes wide. "That's what you're focusing on? And how do you not know what a – no. *I'm* not going to focus on that. I don't care. I'm not going to find out what makes your world so creepily similar and different to mine, because I'm going to save Trillin and we're both getting out of here before the parasite that's infected her realises what a massive fucking mistake it's made."

Ros shook her head. "It's *magic*. It doesn't have a mind. It can't make mistakes. It just ... *is*."

"It might not have before. But now? Trillin isn't human. She's from a species that devours everything it finds. You think you have it bad now, being forced into playing fairy tales? At least you have a way out. If this parasite takes over everything Trillin is, there won't be anywhere left for you to escape to. And if she destroys it first—"

If Trillin absorbed the magical parasite into herself, then she wouldn't be Trillin anymore. And what she became would have all her power and knowledge and all the parasite's desire to take this fairy tale bullshit to a thousand other worlds.

Sian had seen Trillin merge with other parts of the Endless twice. Once, she had attacked a belligerent fragment and in the fight absorbed some of it. Sian hadn't realised it at the time but she'd shed the other fragment so quickly there had to be a reason behind it. The same had happened when she'd merged with Bunny. The two had pulled themselves apart as soon as it was safe.

She'd been merged with the other fragment for a matter of seconds. With Bunny for a minute, maybe less. How long had she been fighting for existence as the parasite crept into her brain the way it had crept into Sian's?

Trillin wanted to be herself. A kinder, less murderous version of everything she had ever been. A version that discovered new ways to be without having to strip that knowledge from the minds of other living things.

And Sian had no magic of her own to help her. Just the raw

emptiness inside her, and the parasite clawing at her skin from the inside and the outside both.

No magic. Unless…

Cold gripped her. Her silent vow from the day she'd first set foot on this world came back to her.

If someone has to kill to get us out of here – I'll do it.

Oh, god, she wished Trillin were here. Which was ridiculous, wasn't it? She'd known her for all of five minutes. There were so many other people she'd lost that she'd known for so much longer. But here, with fate staring her in the face, all she wanted was the strange, sweet creature-woman who'd plucked herself from the devouring Endless to be with her.

And even if everything went right, she might never see her again.

She spun and stormed out the doors, fast so she wouldn't have time to rethink.

"Where are you going?" someone called from behind her.

"To save the world."

It wasn't the whole truth. Sounded good, though. So long as she didn't say the last bit out loud.

Because the only way she could think of to save this world was by damning herself.

Okay, no. That was a lie. She could think of two ways to save this world.

And they both sucked.

Victor caught up with her at the car.

"Don't follow me." Her voice was so stony, she sounded – like him, actually.

"You appear to be stealing my car."

"Borrowing. And you don't want to come with me. Trust me."

He leant close to her, inspecting her face. She stopped herself from snarling at him.

Just.

"You look like a person who's about to make a bad decision," he said mildly.

This time she did snarl at him. "Don't follow me, then."

"I think I will." He slid into the passenger seat before she could stop him. "Where are we going?"

She thought of the university campus, its patchwork of buildings from different styles and eras, and the enchanted halls that in her world lay beneath it. She owed it to something to go and check. Herself, probably.

She thought of what lay beyond the campus, to damp student flats and old villas half-mouldering on the cold side of the valley, and turned the other way. Back to the peninsula.

It was a great day for it. Clear skies. Bright sun. Every time she caught a glint of golden light bouncing off a window or another car, she flinched.

"I expect I'm going to regret asking this." Victor turned his face to the sun and scowled at it. "How does magic work in your world?"

Sian was grateful for the distraction. The time between having an idea and finding out whether it would work was always excruciating. And if this didn't work—

"Don't get too excited," she told him, hands tight on the wheel. "Mostly it ends up getting you killed."

He blinked. So did she. That was ... not what she'd expected to say.

"What do you mean by that?"

What *did* she mean by that? She licked dry lips.

Mostly it ends up getting you killed. Usually when she let her mouth run, it spouted bullshit.

This was a really inconvenient time for it to suddenly tell the truth.

"Magic always has a high attrition rate. Everyone knows someone who blew themselves up, or tore themselves to pieces, or if they were lucky, got cursed into a tree or a toad or something. This one family back home, they made a tradition of it. Making sure they fell afoul of a curse before something worse happened to them."

"Something worse being?"

She clutched for meaning as she tried to describe the world she'd come from and, in doing so, was forced to look at it from the outside for the first time. Even with Trillin she hadn't had to introduce her to how things worked, because Trillin had all the memories the Endless made during its incursions into her Earth. Which was part of the problem, wasn't it?

"Magic is something we use. It's not like here, all eaten up by a parasite that picks you and turns you into a puppet for whatever fucked-up story it's telling. We use magic. How could you not? We soak in it every moment we're alive, breathing it in, and you can do *anything* if you can figure out how. Find out secrets about the world no one ever knew before. Create new things no one's ever seen. Change yourself, if you want to." She took a deep breath. "And eventually, something goes wrong, and it gets you. When I was growing up, we used to have this group of family friends who had kids around the same ages as my sister and me. They'd drag us out for barbecues and picnics and let us all run wild. And then people started dropping off. No one really talked about it, after the funerals. It happens to everyone, so why mention it? And – and then our parents died, too."

In a car accident, she added silently, as though that meant anything.

"Bit hard to get to the picnics after that. Our aunt took us in, but—" She gritted her teeth, waiting for the light to change. "You said normal people here don't see magic. That they won't even notice that dragon corpse when it's right in front of their nose. At home – well, they see it. But they don't understand. My Aunt Nel isn't magical. Neither's Flora. My sister. She fucked off overseas as soon as she could. I mean, you would, wouldn't you? Losing your parents and not even having magic to make it—"

Worth it, she didn't say.

"—to make it make sense."

"Does it make sense?"

"Course it does. It's the way things work."

He shot her a sidelong glance. "That definitely sounds like you using magic, and not the other way around."

"It's no different than driving a car. Everyone drives. Everyone knows someone who's been in an accident."

"And yet the leading cause of death among motorists manages not to be motor accidents. You make it sound like every magic-user in your world dies from it."

But, she wanted to say, except she didn't have anything to say afterwards. But what? "It's not that bad."

It's worse, a treacherous voice said deep inside her head.

Victor's voice was careful. "I'm sorry about your parents."

"Thanks."

"Could be worse, anyway," she said to break the horrifying silence that loomed up after that. Victor made a doubtful noise. "I'm serious. It *has* been worse. That's why we have the university. It … slows things down. You have to do paperwork, and ethics approvals, and get official sign-off for anything even slightly exciting. And most people survive it." She hesitated. "They probably think I'm dead, though."

"You know." Victor's voice was almost wistful. "I thought I was going to regret asking you that question for a whole different reason."

You don't know the half of it. Neither had she, until she'd had to turn the idea around in her head and see all the holes in it and all the ways it might work, and what it meant that she had this idea at all. The sort of person she had to be to have come up with it. The sort of person her world had made her.

If you can do it, why not? It'll catch up to us all sooner or later. What's a little sooner?

And then, all too soon, they arrived.

It wasn't the winding Portobello drive that had left her feeling queasy this time. Or the tug of Trillin's – the Evil Queen's – proximity, this close to the castle.

She stared down at the pocket-sized lawn. The tiny beach. The gleaming, bloody corpse.

Not as gleaming, now. *I guess it has been a few days.* Still bloody, but stale and browned. But what made Sian stop and grimace was the way it was already rotting in on itself, sides caving in, scaled skin stretched over empty bones. "Has something been eating it?"

Victor glanced at it begrudgingly, hands thrust deep in his pockets. "It's not needed anymore. After you kill them, they … disintegrate. Slowly."

Which didn't answer her question. Sian moved in closer, realising with a distant part of her mind that this was just another way of distracting herself from what she had to do next, but unable to stop herself. Something *had* been eating it.

The world itself, maybe.

The air around the dragon felt less scraped-clean than it had when it was freshly dead. Whale fall, Sian thought, and eventually her brain hunted out why.

It was another one of those things Flora had told her. She was starting to feel uneasy about how often her sister was coming to mind, especially while she was determinedly not thinking about how their parents had died, and most of their friends, and quite a few of the kids she'd grown up with, now that she thought about it.

When a dead whale fell to the ocean floor, it became an ecosystem. Food source and habitat all in one.

The dead dragon was magic, and now that it was dead, that magic was getting out again.

If she did what Ros and Victor expected her to do – picked out a princess and let her brain explode out her ears – would the magic leave Trillin? Would the parasite's control over her disintegrate, the same way this creature was falling apart now that its purpose was complete?

No. She'd made her decision. And she couldn't risk that it was *only* this world's magic that would dissolve from Trillin if she took herself out of the picture.

"Is that why we're here?" Victor asked. "You said you'd need more power to get back to your own world. Are you going to use the dragon to … refuel?"

He sounded sick. Fair enough. But the answer was no. She needed magic, but not to escape. And the magic she needed wasn't the dragon. It might be dead, but the magic that had brought it into existence wasn't. And, importantly, it was this world's magic. Magic that had spent who fucking knew how long being recycled through the parasite's happy-ever-after engine.

Rolling around in it like a dog that had found the world's biggest and stinkiest dead seal sounded like a good recipe for going full sword-wielding lunatic.

But the dragon wasn't the only magic here.

She crouched beside the body. This close, it was even more obvious that the dragon was dissolving. Its scales were pitted and frayed. The edges of the slash wound along its throat were soft and frilly-looking, like baked-on food scraps left to soak too long in the sink.

She swallowed hard, and told her stomach not to do anything embarrassing. "Hey, Vic. Can I borrow some clothes after this?"

"Why? Wait. What are you doing? You're not seriously – ugh."

Ugh was about right. Sian aimed herself at where she thought the escape pod had been, and started digging.

It was drier than she'd expected. Not that she'd thought about what it would be like before she started. The rustle of what were once scales, brushing against one another. Flesh that crumpled like beehive cardboard where once it had pulsed and flexed and bled. Bones that left a residue like ash on her forearms.

The magic was the real problem. It itched against her skin, looking for a way in. Or maybe it was her skin that itched to let it in, so parched it would soak in poison so long as it was wet.

And if she let it, then what? *Stop thinking*, she told herself, but it was too late. Would throwing herself at the mercy of this world's abandoned magic be the same as letting it seek her out? Would there be any of herself left if she let it soak into her from all around like this, or would she be like Victor had said, a helpless scream trapped behind her own eyes as she acted the prince?

The hero. Someone who did good in the world.

Instead of what she was planning now.

Her world hadn't forged her to be a prince. It had made her something else. The parasite should have paid more attention to who it was infecting.

"If you'd told me this was what you were planning I could have given you my gardening gloves!" Victor sounded aggrieved. It wasn't like he was the one digging around in dead dragon. "A shovel! A – a trowel!"

But that would have slowed her down, and she couldn't afford to slow down.

The corpse didn't weigh as much as it should have, either. After a few minutes she was able to shoulder it out of the way. Half of it, anyway. The remains of the escape pod lay beneath. Shattered, but…

Not as broken as she'd expected. Again, as much as she'd allowed herself to expect anything.

The physical structure had splintered under the dragon's weight. The walls were a maze of sharp lines snapped and piled in on themselves. What had once been windows hung in the air like kaleidoscopes, still fracturing piece by piece as though pressure was still twisting down on them.

The magic was splintered, too. A bird's nest of razor blades. Slightly nibbled on.

Sian's heart fell.

Her hunch had been right.

Trillin was afraid.

Not for herself. The attrition of herself against the parasite's ceaseless covetous curiosity didn't scare her anymore. At least not since she'd figured out what it was. What its presence meant.

And her thoughts kept going to how Sian had looked at her in those last moments before her body was no longer her own. She'd seen that expression on many humans' faces, when she had been part of the Endless.

But she could handle that. She knew it was only this world's magic, and that Sian would fight it with every fibre of her being.

It was everything else she'd seen reflected in her beloved's eyes that made fear writhe through her. And everything she hadn't seen. When Sian came after her, to save her, and lost.

Sian was fighting. But she was desperate. Trillin had seen what the humans of Sian's world did when they were desperate. The lengths they would go to protect what they cared for.

It was so close to what the Endless was. What it would do, to protect what was its own.

Don't, she wanted to cry out to Sian across the scoured air that separated them. *Don't do it. Don't hurt yourself like that.*

Don't become what I once was.

Sian scratched on a length of splintered wall. A moment later, a small, furry face appeared.

"Sweek?"

"Hi, Bunny."

What were you, once?

The voice flowed and flowered, smearing her own thoughts before she could form them. She felt it puzzling over their remains.

It wasn't talking with her mouth now, she noted. All its attention was inwards. Towards her.

You still don't know what I was? she asked it. *What I am? What you took over?*

You keep it from me. An uneasiness echoed around her.

Of course I do. She hesitated. *And what about what you once were?*

I was ... not. I had to ensure – to make others become... The voice veered away from something, as though avoiding pain.

It will be better. You will be better. Everything will be better. There was something like desperation in the voice now. Not the desperation of someone trying to convince themselves of what they were saying, but of putting up words like a wall between them and something that threatened to strip them down to the bone.

What are you hiding? she asked it, and showed it how easily she could find out the answer for herself.

Not yet, though. Not until she had no other options.

She wasn't who, or what, she had once been. She'd made a new way for herself.

And Sian—

She had to find a way out of this before Sian made a new way for herself, too.

Or what? the being asked.

Or – she began, but it was too late. Batting questions back and forth had created a chink in her defenses; too much curiosity.

Or, perhaps, too much impatience, from the parts of her that remembered what she had once been. Not a prisoner in her own body. Not careful and guarded and losing more of herself minute by minute.

It found a way in.

Bunny was magic.

Endless magic. It was a fragment, same as Trillin. A bubble of individuality that would have merged back with the Endless's single consciousness via being eaten by another, much larger fragment, except Sian had grabbed it and stuffed it down her shirt before that could happen.

She'd saved it. And then it had saved her and Trillin, incidentally or coincidentally or basically by accident. As though saying it was by accident made it less of a big deal that Bunny had saved all their lives.

Because Bunny had Earth magic, too. It had nibbled through Sian's belongings and furniture and the walls of her home, and had absorbed the magic of her world as effectively as a witch rolling around in a herb garden.

And what had been absorbed could be squeezed out again.

Sian needed magic. Trillin needed her to have magic.

Bunny had magic.

Even she could do that maths.

"Sweek!" Bunny butted against a glittering constellation of broken windowpane, gnawed a hole big enough to squeeze through, and leapt into Sian's outstretched hands.

She backed up through the broken shards of their portal room, past the dissolving remnants of the dead dragon. Victor said something, but she wasn't listening.

Bunny was a trembling, writhing double handful of puffy fur and little scrabbly claws and oddly placed eyeballs. Like Trillin, it moved through various forms, but this was the sort of thing it appeared to prefer: small and fuzzy.

Brimming with borrowed power.

Her fingers tightened involuntarily. If she wanted this power, it wouldn't be airy-fairy absorption. It would be taking. Stripping, scouring away, like she'd done to her own body already until her bones were raw and cracking.

Like the magic here had done to its entire world.

No wonder she felt sick.

Trillin had given up her entire world to be with her. Sure, that world would have devoured her the moment it noticed she existed outside of itself. But until Sian blundered in and drew the Endless's attention irrevocably to them, she'd been safe. Safe enough. Safer than she'd been in any of the wonderful, dangerous time they'd spent together.

Sian would do whatever it took to save Trillin. Anything at all.

And then what? a treacherous voice inside her asked. *After you've wrung every drop out of it?*

Why do you think the easy way will work?

"What's that?" Victor hunched his way over to look over her shoulder. "Is that your idea?"

She buried her face in Bunny's floss-like fur, and when she raised her head again, her eyes were dry.

"Nah," she said. "Here. You take it. I've got something else I need to do first."

First. Hah. Like she would be able to do anything afterwards.

She would do anything to save Trillin. That was what she kept telling herself.

It was time to put it to the test.

Sian pressed on, through trees that clustered so close together she had to climb to find space between their branches, feet crunching on a road that turned to loose stones when she looked at it, and asphalt when she didn't. Or maybe it was both and neither, all of the time and none of the time.

The sense of magic grew thicker. But not the *feel* of magic. All the magic of this world was still inaccessible to her. And for a few more minutes, it had to stay that way.

The castle lay ahead of her. It was fighting her off at the same time it drew her closer – but that was part of the story too, wasn't it?

Fucking stories.

She found herself swinging her empty hand at a tangle of thorns as though it held a sword, and for a moment, felt the blade's weight.

Why are you fighting it?

Sian froze, one hand flat against the tree she'd been about to duck around. For a moment, she stared helplessly at the mottled trunk, as though it was the tree that had spoken.

It was, in a way. Magic was all around her. She wasn't heading towards the parasite. She was in it already, and the voice spoke to her from every leaf and branch.

Oh, Trillin, she thought, her heart fracturing in her chest.

"Fighting what?" she said, and the leaves danced all around her.

Your happy-ever-after.

Sian swallowed back a snort of disbelief. "I'm good, thanks. No happy-ever-after required. Just let Trillin go, and we'll leave you to whatever fucked-up game you're playing here."

You are so afraid, the voice told her. *Alone in a strange world. Betrayed by everything you thought you knew about yourself. Your world. Your people.*

"I'm only afraid because you stole my girlfriend," Sian said, and almost cried. Great. Wonderful. She could say it to a magical parasite, but not to the woman herself?

And now she would never have the chance.

Keep fighting, she told herself, as the woods froze around her.

The forest rustled. *You don't need to be alone*, the voice told her. *Let me help you. You cannot have this one. She isn't right for you.*

"You—"

You don't need to be afraid. I will give you someone who will never change so much you fall out of love with them.

Little shivers raced across Sian's skin. "What are you talking about? I'm not scared of how Trillin changes. I like – I *love* it about her. And I will love seeing who she becomes. Who she *chooses* to become, not infected by whatever you're doing to her. Someone she discovers by herself."

With you at her side.

"Yes, and—"

Making sure she becomes the right sort of person.

"That's not—"

I've seen it in her mind already. How much your approval means to her. How she longs to make your eyes light up.

A pause.

Oh god, Sian thought. *It's seen her mind. Am I too late, after all?*

Bipedalism. Fingers that touch gently, instead of curling around and around. That intricate cocktail of nerves and sensory receptors and display that lets you enjoy how she lets you make her feel...

"Stop it!"

And suddenly she was on her knees, hands bloodied as she caught herself on broken stone. A staircase. She looked up. This wasn't any of her country's so-called castles. It was a turret spearing the sky, a narrow stone staircase winding all the way around it to the top.

And at the top, something glowed with the same gold she'd learnt to distrust.

Sian got to her feet and started to climb, and the magic pressed in all around her, frustrated and gleeful at the same time.

She'd come here expecting the Queen, the parasite, to be the same as she'd left it. Contained within the body it had stolen. But this was ... different. As though the winter surrounding her wasn't just a halo effect of the Queen's presence, the same way Ros's tower smelled like roses, but *was* the Queen. The parasite.

It was like walking through the Endless.

Was any part of it still Trillin? If the parasite knew her thoughts – how much of her had it taken? How much was left?

Her lungs were full of ice. Each step made her bones grate together.

This wasn't plain exhaustion, and it wasn't something the parasite was doing to her, either. It was her own body existing somewhere it didn't belong.

Betrayed by everything she thought she knew about herself.

Hah.

She reached the top of the stairs. Trillin was there, lying on her back on a stone plinth like a tomb.

Sian walked slowly towards her, listing caveats in her mind. The parasite was all around her, so this wasn't necessarily Trillin. Or even what was left of her. It could as easily be a construction. A body built using Trillin's knowledge, on the same lines she preferred.

She crept closer. The figure's chest rose and fell, as though Trillin was the sort of person who needed to breathe.

Still. This was how the story went, wasn't it? She bent her head, standing beside her, and wasn't surprised to find a sword in her hand as she did so.

"I'm going to save her," she said out loud. The words were awkward on her tongue. "I'm going to take her away, now, and you're going to let us go."

She stared down at the body on the plinth. Trillin's form was so light, all floating limbs and trailing edges. If she didn't hold her tight, she would fall through her fingers.

Look at that, the voice mused. *A ribcage. What a useful thing. Solid bones. An impermeable outer layer. Don't worry. You won't drop her like this. She knows what you enjoy – a solid form to hold onto.*

"I'd love her no matter what she looked like. Or felt like. And you're wrong. She isn't – she doesn't—"

Reshape herself to please me. Except she had, hadn't she? She'd become more humanoid each time they met. And Sian *did* love the way she reacted to her touch, her excitement, her happiness...

She will make herself everything you dream of. The voice twisted inside her, finding pinholes in the armor guarding her heart. *She'll become what you want of her, and then she'll stop.*

"No."

What? Don't you like that? But you said you wanted her back. Which is it that you like the least, the voice pondered. *That she will stop changing – or that you won't? Nothing holds your interest for long, does it? That's why you've persevered so greatly in the short time you've been here. You know it won't be long before your attention flits away, as it does every time. Never staying in one place long enough to truly love whatever caught your eye. This little scrap of the Endless has entertained you so far ... but what will happen to her when your interest wanes? When she's remade herself in your image and you move on?*

Her breath stuck in her throat. This wasn't what she'd come here expecting to face. "That won't happen."

Let me make you a hero, and you will be forever faithful. You will never hurt her.

Lungs empty, chest aching, Sian stared down at Trillin.

Never hurt her.

"You'd make me a prince, and her my princess? You said – you said you'd make her a princess. I just want to be sure. You'd make her *my* princess?" She hesitated. "I didn't think that was possible. Isn't she – you saw her and you took her for a monster."

Anything is possible, with love, said the voice. Soft. Convincing.

"I'll be a prince, a hero, and she'll be a princess?"

If you stopped fighting it, you would see that you were a hero already.

Normally, her mind would be whirring at this point. The absence of it itched, the ghost of a thousand lightning-forked thoughts. Distractible. Feckless.

But this time, her mind was quiet. Nothing distracted her from what she must do.

"All right," she said, the words falling out of her like stones. "Make her a princess. And I'll stop fighting."

Magic sang all around her, golden on her brow and silver in her hand. It sang until her soul shivered with it. Her eyes opened to a world that suddenly made sense.

Then she closed them, and followed the lilting path of magic-song to its source.

Yeah, the magic was all around her. And inside, now, too. It found whatever part of her made her a witch in her own world and seeded something of itself in it.

Oh. Hah. Not a parasite, after all.

It took hold of her slowly, gently, this time, like a lover. Or someone trying not to startle a horse. Sian bit back a sigh of relief. This thing was never going to turn Trillin into a princess. It needed her. And it was like Ros and Victor said: if it needed Trillin, it needed Sian safely out of the way.

It was trying to get Sian out of the way. Logically, that meant there must still be enough of Trillin left for it to be keeping her away from. And even if all of it had merged with all of her – Trillin had made herself once already, stripping away everything she didn't want to be. Given the chance, she could do it again.

Sian's lips moved as she stared with her mind's eye into the magic taking root inside her.

"You're wrong," she said, the sound of it a long way away. "I'm not afraid that I'll change, and become someone who forgets what Trillin means to me. I'm worried I won't. I'm worried I'll stay what my world made me, and never be anything else. I'm worried Trillin will hate me for this and I'll never have the chance to hear her tell me so."

Her voice shook too much to sound princely, and she didn't know who she was trying to talk to. The magic, or Trillin, or herself. "I was never meant to be a hero."

But you can be.

"Maybe."

It almost had her.

"But – you were wrong. About all of it. Trillin isn't the monster. And I'm really not a hero."

She wouldn't tear Bunny to pieces to save Trillin. But she would do this.

She gripped the magic where it had anchored itself in her soul, and it stopped singing.

The world held still, trapped in an enchantment that had burnt every scrap of magic that had ever existed here.

The magic, the voice, wasn't a parasite after all. It was a spell. An old one, built on itself over and over, always the same thing. A princess, to be rescued; a prince, to do the rescuing; and between them, the fulcrum on which they each depended and that, once destroyed, sent them hurtling into inescapable orbit around each other. The wolf, the dragon, the witch, the monstrous queen crowned with shards of broken stars.

Something to kill, so you could stop being afraid. Something real to defeat, to bring to an end, so all your own suffering would fall away.

Take that fulcrum away, and what happened?

Something had to take its place. Like when Victor killed the dragon and Trillin was right there to take the next swing of the axe.

There would always be a monster. Something easy to defeat.

Something to make sure star-crossed lovers found each other and stayed that way.

Why? If this was a spell, where had it come from? Who would cast something like this?

She held the strangling roots tighter, seeking. The spell wanted to change who she was. But that went both ways. Maybe the poor bastards who lived here didn't know that. Maybe only she could have done it – a witch from another world.

The same way the spell had found what made her, she found what made it.

Magic collapsed all around, pulling her down.

Behind the voice, behind the magic, behind the spell, was a story. Her mind showed it to her as a book, but she knew that trick. A protective measure. The spell protecting itself and her brain protecting her – well, fuck that.

The words wriggled and writhed in front of her eyes as mud dripped up her legs, cold and clinging, and the sky broke into a thousand pieces above.

They're all dead, somebody screamed and cried and whimpered. *He's dead. Oh, god, he's dead.*

In the space between flashes in the broken sky, when all the light was gone and all the warmth stolen, in the mud and the fear and the darkness and the pain, she found a wish inscribed on a still-beating heart.

The words were so familiar, and another piece of the puzzle fell silently into place.

She looked down at the body whose memory she'd stolen into, and saw one hand stretched out to where another had been, before the sky came roaring down on them. Bloodied and bruised and beaten. Magic hadn't been enough to save them. Love hadn't. Everything he'd been too afraid to fear had come true.

The sky opened again, raining steel and fire.

This can't be it. Let us have a happy end. Not this. Please, not this.

Death had sealed the spell. Made it something nobody had expected. Not even this long-dead sorcerer, grieving and hoping as magic stopped his heart before anything else could. His dying cry had echoed out into the world, harvesting all the magic it could find as the spell tried to fulfil a hopeless wish. It had found form in the stories humans told themselves. It had stamped lives into happy shapes, over and over again.

And when people fought back, Ros and her tower of princesses, Victor and the woman he couldn't be near without their love twisting them into something they didn't want to be – the spell needed to change.

And it found Trillin, who changed herself so much.

Why make monster after monster when *one* could last forever? The voice was a whisper in the mud around her ankles, the final heartbeat trembling beneath her fingers as she pressed her hand against the spell book. A Queen who could rise wherever she was needed, her power a web across the world.

Sian could see it. It looked a lot like everything Trillin had tried to leave behind.

"But you got stuck here too, didn't you?" That was why the air around the rotting dragon had been heavy with magic. Trapped in Trillin's body, the spell hadn't been able to scoop it up. "You've made yourself into the monster this world needs to make sure everyone else gets their happy ending. You wanted to doom Trillin, and you've doomed yourself with her."

It didn't like that.

Viciousness gathered on Sian's tongue like poison. *You don't like it?* she wanted to snarl. *What about all the people whose lives you've destroyed, forcing them into happy-ever-afters? What about all the magic of this world, tied up in your endless enchantment? What about every charm and spell and miracle that might have been, if some poor bastard hadn't wished that the world was a better place in the seconds before he died?*

But she couldn't find it in herself to judge it, or the long-dead sorcerer who had sparked it.

Not when she was here, holding the world's magic in her fist, and about to do something even worse.

Victor said that when a princess found her prince, the monsters left them alone.

Things were getting metaphysical. She was the sorcerer knee-deep in mud and blood and grief. She was Sian, standing in front of a body that looked like Trillin's. She was an intruder, peeling away the layers of this thing the spell had become, and seeing what else lay on the stone tomb.

She was a prince. Exactly the way it wanted her to be.

She put down her sword. You always put down your sword, first. By this point, you didn't need it anymore.

Would never need it again.

She hoped.

Trillin wanted to not have to kill anything else, and this was the only way Sian could see of making that happen.

She knelt in front of Trillin's still form. The fine cilia on her cheeks rippled. It was more convincing than her chest moving as though there were lungs in it.

She's sleeping, Sian told herself. As if in response to her thought, the cilia began to fray, feathering out into fine strands like the fronds of a delicate seaweed.

Princess. The title didn't fit. Trillin could change her shape a thousand times and there would still be too much of her to fit in that box.

Not that that mattered. The spell pressed in all around and within her, waiting for Sian to hold up her end of the bargain.

She closed her eyes and spared a last moment's thought for the world she was leaving behind. Ros and her determination not to let the hand of fate choose someone unsuitable for either her or her tenants. Victor, trapped in the long-distance relationship of his nightmares. Bunny – ahh, fuck, she'd left Bunny with Victor. Oh well. At least he'd have someone to grumble to.

And maybe this would help fix things for all of them, after all.

Or it would make things worse. She regretted that possibility.

Not enough to stop, though.

With one final thought for the poor bastard whose dying wish had got them all into this mess, she reached out, let the magic in—

Her spine straightened. She was out there, somewhere, the woman whose heart called to hers like birdsong across a mountain valley. The monster was slain; her princess awaited.

Out there.

Far away.

"No," Sian whispered, as gold clamped around her forehead. "She's right here."

And she lifted the heart that anchored the spell from Trillin's chest. Not Trillin herself, not any part of her – but the spell that had trapped itself within her.

If she was going to be a prince, this would be her princess.

"You made yourself part of the story," she told it, as the dead sorcerer's final heartbeat pulsed again and again beneath her fingers. "An Evil Queen. Powerful. Endless." She took a deep breath as magic delved into the deepest regions of her soul, finding the shape of her and changing it to fit. Her vision filmed and sparkled, like gold dust was filling the air and coating everything around her.

Including the heart of the Evil Queen.

One last chance to make things right. "That isn't how this is going to end. My monster's already slain. If she's not dead yet, she will be soon. Which means I'm here to save you. *Princess.*"

The spell recoiled, but it was too late; it had run these paths too many times before. A prince had a princess.

And when they found each other, there was no need for monsters anymore.

Her princess. Sian's vision filmed over again and she wasn't holding a heart in her hands anymore; she was holding the Evil Queen, her perfect face gilded with magic. She was holding a dead man, his body bleeding gold instead of red, holding misery and hope and rage and her own heart torn out of her chest.

For one brief moment she was holding Trillin, her eyes a constellation beyond any earthly jewels, and then the magic let her go. It didn't need a monster anymore. Her role was fulfilled.

Trillin disappeared. *She's safe*, Sian thought, and let go of the last pieces of herself the magic hadn't touched yet.

The Queen was in her arms. No longer a queen. Not evil. Staring up at her in confusion and wonder, this lost enchantment that had scoured the world of all its magic, conjured up creatures and monsters to be slain, forged together the hearts of princes and princesses so they would never know the pain that had created it, and now had a body of its own. Not the one it had stolen and discovered to be a trap. A body of its own. Blood and flesh and warmth.

And gold.

Her one, true love.

Her happy ending.

Its happy ending, too.

The Princess's brow furrowed adorably. "My prince?"

"My princess."

The words tasted like happiness. Like this perfect moment would never end. The prince cupped her hand around the princess's cheek and leant down to kiss her.

A tentacle wrapped itself around her wrist and jerked it away.

Trillin stared into Sian's eyes, glazed not with fear, but with perfect happiness.

She was herself again. She *had* her self again, all her mass and thoughts and every memory she'd ever made or taken. And she knew exactly what Sian was doing.

She was giving her a way out.

The spell was caught in its own happy-ever-after and all the magic hat had gone into fulfilling its purpose was spilling back into the world. It was the opposite of the cataclysmic spell Trillin had taken apart to build the portal room and escape Sian's world; that was death, and this was life. Sian was offering it to her.

Trillin could use it to leave. To go anywhere. And Sian would stay here, trapped forever in this one, perfect moment.

She'd been afraid of the wrong thing. Sian hadn't sacrificed anything or anyone to save her.

Except herself.

The joy in Sian's eyes now wasn't Sian's joy. It wasn't the glee that bubbled irrepressibly from her lungs and eyes when she figured something out. It wasn't the red flush of pleasure that crashed like waves over her skin when they touched. It wasn't even the gentle glow, lighting her like a candled egg, that she had only rarely glimpsed in quiet moments. And there had been so few quiet moments.

If she took the safety Sian was offering, there would be no more moments of any kind. She would never see any of those joys again. Sian would never experience them again.

She would only have ... this.

This *ending*.

More tentacles whipped out, quicker than thought. They wrapped around Sian's limbs and tore her away from the golden enchantment, away from the promise and curse of the kiss hanging on her lips.

The spell broke. It snapped out across the world.

The queen pushed herself up on perfect white arms, her golden eyes sharpening. The balance was tipping. Trapped in Trillin's body, she'd become one thing. Caught in the orbit of the spell's version of love, she'd been another. Almost. But now, that spell was broken, fragmenting.

Which of them would play the monster when it made itself whole again?

Sian turned her head and buried it against Trillin's body. "Are you *rescuing* me?" Her voice was effervescent with a thousand layers of feelings Trillin didn't have names for, and some she did. Wonder. Relief. The tiniest hint of resentment.

And joy. More than anything else, joy.

Trillin tightened her grip on her beloved. "Not quite," she said, making new mouths to smile with as Sian's eyes lit with the gentlest warmth. All the magic in the world was rushing back towards them. Compared to that flood, it would only take a little to do what she needed to do.

"You're not going to kill her. I don't know if you even can, but—" Sian's hands twined through her tendrils. "You don't have to. I found a way where you don't have to."

"Sacrificing yourself?"

Sian smiled weakly. "I considered blowing up the entire world. Making myself the baddest monster of them all. Figured you wouldn't like that, though."

"I don't like this plan, either."

"I mean, same. But I was kind of running out of options." She hesitated. "And time. I think. I don't – it's all a bit wobbly?"

Trillin stared down at her, and did more than stare. Tiny sensory filaments on her tendrils told her more than any number of eyes could. Sian's heart rate was too fast, her skin too cool. Each breath took more effort and brought less air than the last. "You're hurt."

"It's not much of a sacrifice if I'm almost used up already, huh? Hahaha. Ha…" She pressed her face against Trillin again and some of the tension racking her body dissipated. "I'm out of fuel. My world's magic. I didn't realise I needed it like this. I thought – thought we used magic. Or it uses us. Victor makes a good point, really. Like those seeds that need to be shat out by birds to sprout. But – but we need it going through us, like air…"

"You need to go home."

"I need you to get the hell out of this dimension before it steals you from me again."

"Then the solution is simple." The queen was rising, now, still tipping the balance between villain and victim.

Or something else. No princess ever looked at her loyal knight the way the queen was looking at Sian. Maybe, when the magic all came spilling back, it wouldn't return to this new being at all. Maybe she would stay something new.

Trillin wasn't afraid. The spell hadn't reformed itself yet and, until it did, the only danger here was her. She could destroy this whole world. She'd spent the whole time she'd been here trying not to – but she could.

How simple it would be.

She pressed her mouth against Sian's forehead.

"I hope you have a plan," Sian said. "I'm out."

"I do." She wrapped herself more closely around her beloved. "I'm stealing you away. Like monsters do."

Sian's Earth. Trillin remembered so many versions of it. Every human the Endless had taken from this world experienced it differently. Every fragment of the Endless that had made its way here, too.

But this experience was all her own.

Building another pocket universe had been simple. This time, she paid more attention to where she landed it. She found a sun-swept hillside far from any other humans, and carried Sian out with one arm pressed against her own eyes, so that she wouldn't see Trillin and go mad with terror.

They lay together on bronzed tussocks, watching the sun set. At least, Trillin was watching it. And watching Sian. They'd talked a little, wondering what would happen to that other Earth now the spell that had twisted its natural magic was broken. Sian tried to hide it, but Trillin could tell she was worried she'd made it worse.

"Worse than a spell that wanted to control everyone it touched, forever?" Trillin asked.

Sian groaned.

Her breathing had calmed the moment her lungs filled with the air of her own Earth. Her heartbeat had evened out; sweat was cooling on her skin, and not being replaced. Being here was healing her.

But her eyes were still shut fast, and a muscle twitched beneath her left eye whenever a breeze sent tussock fronds wafting against her skin.

"I hate this," Sian admitted in a shamed undertone.

Trillin stilled. "Why?"

"It's working. I'm already feeling better. And that means I *have* to be here. That no matter how far we manage to go together, we'll always have to come back. Here, where I can't even look at you. Where – where you remember killing so many people like me. I don't want that for us."

Her voice was raw. Trillin wanted to smooth it over, make Sian whole again the way Sian had made sure she could be whole again.

But humans didn't work like that.

"You're part of this world."

"Yeah. More than I realised. I mean, obviously it's *my* world, but I'm... I belong to it, as well?" Her eyebrows furrowed as she waved one hand, seeking the words to describe the ideas roiling inside her mind. "Like – like I'm some key part of the magical ecology. I'm not just … me." She jerked her head as though she was about to glance up at Trillin's face, remembered, and swore. One arm slung over her eyes again, she continued. "Did you know this about me? About humans here?"

"No. I didn't know." And that should have been a good thing. She'd learnt something new. Something she didn't already know through conquest.

Except if she *had* already known, she could have told Sian.

"What's the matter?" Sian murmured. "You're rippling. Little pointy spikes, all over."

"Sorry—"

"No, they're great. But something's wrong." Sian nestled closer against her, one hand tangling in the cloud of feathery tendrils she was wearing like hair. "Tell me."

Trillin told her.

Sian hesitated for a moment, then said, "Wouldn't have made a difference. I still would have used everything I could, trying to get you back."

"I don't want—"

"I don't want to lose you. Or even get close to losing you. Not again. And if you were about to say you don't want me to get myself hurt saving you, well, too bad. I'll always throw myself in to help you.

I love you," she said, the words tumbling out of her as she twisted her body around so she could touch Trillin's face with both hands, eyebrows high and expressive over eyelids still tightly screwed shut. "I love you, Trillin. I don't know how we're going to make this work, but we will."

Trillin stared at her. Her form changed without conscious thought, absorbing the taste of Sian's words on the air, the scent of her body, the rattling sincerity in her voice, and folding it all inside herself. A memory for the very heart of who she was.

She'd almost lost Sian. They'd almost lost each other. Trillin knew what it was to lose someone you loved – she held the memories of thousands of deaths. Thousands of losses.

Experiencing it herself was different.

"I love you, too," Trillin whispered.

The lower half of Sian's face twitched with a sudden gulp of emotion: part glee, part amazement, part hope.

"We'll make it work," Trillin told her. "I don't know how, but we will. One spell changed the course of all magic in that other Earth. There must be a way to stop you from being afraid when you see me." She paused. "To stop *all* of you from being afraid, when you see any of the Endless."

"Was there ever a time when seeing the Endless didn't turn our brains to putty?" Sian asked absently, her hands far more focused than her words. Trillin wriggled, delighting in sensation.

127

"I don't remember," Trillin replied, almost as absently until her words echoed inside her.

"Guess it isn't another spell, then."

"No – Sian, *I don't remember.* I should remember the first time the Endless saw a human screaming, but I don't. The memory isn't there. And if I don't have the memory…"

"Then the Endless doesn't, either. Huh." Sian rolled on top of her, arms braced either side of Trillin's form, eyes closed with only a thin layer of skin between her and the terror they were discussing.

Trillin's body made a heart for itself without her even thinking about it; it made a heartbeat that hammered through everything she was.

"Hmm," Sian said. "What do you think? Should we give it a go? Saving the world?"

Saving the world. Saving *any* world. Something no part of the Endless had ever done before.

With the woman she loved.

The sun was sinking behind the mountains, taking the heat in the air with it. Trillin stared up at the woman lying over her, on her; the woman who'd risked her own soul to give Trillin a chance to be free.

Sian's heart was beating quickly, but it wasn't the frantic clutching at life that had frightened her so much back on that other Earth. Her skin was warm. The fine hairs on her arms and head moved like delicate fronds in the cooling breeze.

"We should attempt to save the world," Trillin said. "…Later."

This time, the kiss, and everything associated with it, went right.

A NOTE FROM THE AUTHOR

I was three quarters of the way through *How to Get a Girlfriend (When You're a Terrifying Monster)* when I realised not only that I was going to write a sequel to Sian and Trillin's story, but that the sequel would swerve sharply away from the two worlds I'd introduced in *How to Get a Girlfriend.* We'd already seen Sian and Trillin explore one another's worlds – now it was time to throw them both somewhere new.

I hope you enjoyed the detour more than they did.

Sometimes it takes leaving everything you thought you knew behind to see it, and yourself, as you really are. Which is where we leave the two of them. *Almost* ready to save the world. In a bit. Any minute now.

Because getting distracted helped so much the last time.

Sian and Trillin will return in a book which has yet to reveal its title to me. If you would like to be kept up to date with the next Monster Girlfriend book and my future projects, you can find me on Instagram @mariecardno, or visit mariecardno.com and sign up to receive my newsletters.

If you enjoyed *How to Get a Date with the Evil Queen*, please consider leaving a review. Reviews and personal recommendations help get books in front of new readers, and are especially important for indie authors.

ACKNOWLEDGEMENTS

This book owes its existence to many people but, above all, to the fact that people actually read book one.

Yes, this still comes as a surprise to me. I wrote *How to Get a Girlfriend (When You're a Terrifying Monster)* as a pandemic stress-reliever, and cheerfully assumed I was only writing for my own amusement. It was the best kind of shock to discover I was wrong. *How to Get a Girlfriend (When You're a Terrifying Monster)* launched to number 6 on the New Zealand Indie Bestseller chart, due to an amazing amount of support from local readers, and the book just... kept selling. To people who kept reading it. All over the world.

My mind? Blown. The fact that I managed to sweep up all the pieces and put it back together in time to write the sequel? For that, I have more people to thank...

Thank you to my husband for supporting me in everything I do and my daughter for being a delightful distraction. To my beta readers – Mel, Kerry, Truis and Amber – for giving me the direction and encouragement I needed. Thank you to my editor, Madeleine, for your razor-sharp expertise. To Laya Rose for another beautiful cover illustration. To everyone on my writerly Slacks and Discords – you know who you are! – for being there when my own enthusiasm ran low and for celebrating with me as *How to Get a Date with the Evil Queen* transformed from something that seemed impossible, to something that strongly resembles a real book.

And thanks, again – because it will always bear repeating – to my readers. It makes me very happy to know that Trillin and Sian have found their people, and that you found them.

ABOUT THE AUTHOR

Marie Cardno grew up in Ōtepoti Dunedin and now lives somewhat further north, halfway between the sea and a French bakery. She writes stories about love, magic, and strange and wonderful worlds.

Marie's debut, *How to Get a Girlfriend (When You're a Terrifying Monster)* won Best Novella at the 2023 Sir Julius Vogel Awards. *How to Get a Date with the Evil Queen* is her second book.

Find Marie online at mariecardno.com.

Milton Keynes UK
Ingram Content Group UK Ltd.
UKHW021452300824
1447UKWH00040B/272